BOOKS BY E. L. KONIGSBURG

Throwing
Shadows

OCT 9 '80

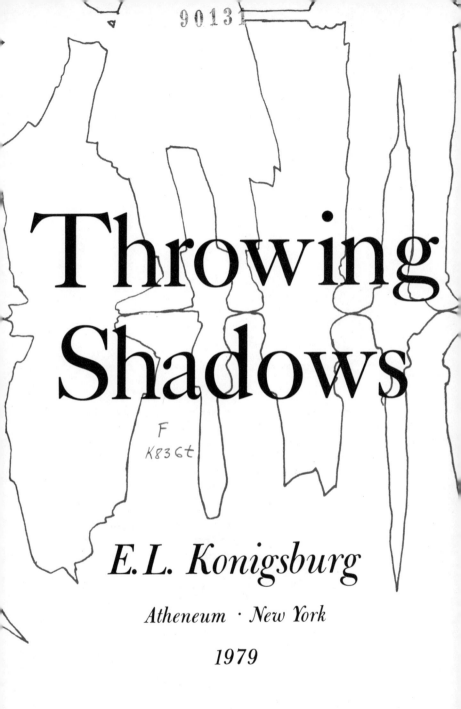

Throwing
Shadows

E. L. Konigsburg

Atheneum · New York

1979

For Fred Sochatoff—
who was there at the beginning,
before either of us knew
it was a beginning

LIBRARY OF CONGRESS CATALOGING IN PUBLICATION DATA

Konigsburg, E. L.   Throwing shadows.

SUMMARY: Five short stories in which young people
gain a sense of Self.
1. Identity—Juvenile fiction.   [1. Identity—
Fiction.   2. Short stories]
PZ7.K8352Th   [Fic]   79-10422
ISBN 0-689-30714-4

Published simultaneously in Canada by
McClelland & Stewart, Ltd.
Manufactured by The Book Press,
Brattleboro, Vermont
Designed by Mary M. Ahern
First Edition

Contents

On Shark's Tooth Beach

by *Ned*

My dad is Hixon of Hixon's Landing, the fishing camp down on the intracoastal waterway just across Highway A1A. Our camp isn't a fancy one. Just two coolers, one for beer and one for bait, plus four boats and eight motors that we rent out.

Dad was raised on a farm in Nebraska, but he joined the Navy and signed on for the war in Vietnam and came back knowing two things. One, he hated war, and two, he loved the sea. Actually, he came back with two loves. The other one was my mother. There wasn't *any* way *any*one could get him to settle *any*where that was far from the ocean when he got out of the service, so he bought this small stretch of land in north Florida, and we've been there for all of my life that I can remember.

Dad's got this small pension for getting wounded over in Nam, so between what we sell, what we rent and what the government sends, we do all right. We're not what you're likely to call rich, but we are all right. Mom doubts that we'll ever make enough money to pay for a trip to her native country of Thailand, but she doesn't seem to mind. She says that it is more important to love where you're at than to love where you're from.

Mom makes and sells sandwiches for the fishermen. She does a right good job on them, I can tell you. There is this about Mom's sandwiches: you don't have to eat halfway through to the middle to find out what's between the bread, and once you get hold of a bite, you don't have to guess at whether it is egg salad or tuna that you're eating. The filling is high in size and in flavor.

The town next door to us is spreading south toward our landing, and both Mom and Dad say that our property will be worth a pretty penny in a few years. But both of them always ask, "What's a pretty penny worth when you can't buy anything prettier than what you already have?" I have to agree. Maybe because I don't know anything else, but I can't imagine what it would be like not to have a sandbox miles and miles long and a pool as big as an ocean for a playground across the street—even if the street is a highway. I can't ever remember going to sleep but that I heard some water shushing and slurping or humming and hollering for a lullaby.

Last spring, just as the days were getting long enough that a person could both start and finish something between the time he got home from school and the time he went to bed, I went out onto our dock and I saw this guy all duded up from a catalogue. Now that the town has grown toward us, we have more of these guys than we used to. When you've been in the business of fishing all your life, you come to know the difference between fishermen and guys who have a hobby. Here are some of the clues:

1. The hat. A real fisherman's hat is darkened along the edges where the sweat from his hand leaves marks. A non-fisherman's hat has perfect little dent marks in it.

2. The smile. Real fishermen don't smile while they're fishing unless someone tells them a joke. Real fishermen wear their faces in the same look people wear when they are in church—deliberate and far-off—the way they do when they don't want to catch the eye of the preacher. The only time that look changes is when they take a swig of beer and then it changes only a little and with a slow rhythm like watching instant replay on television. Non-fishermen twitch their necks around like pigeons, which are very citified birds, and non-fishermen smile a lot.

3. The umbrella. Real fishermen don't have them.

This old guy sat on a wooden-legged, canvas-bottom folding campstool that didn't have any salt burns on it anywhere and put his rod into one of the holders that Dad had set up along the dock railing. Then he held out his hand and called out, "Hey, boy, do you know what I've got here?"

I walked on over to him and said, "Name's Ned."

"What's that?" he asked, cupping his hand over his ear so that the breeze wouldn't blow it past him.

"I said that my name is Ned," I repeated.

"All right, Ed," he said. "I have a question for you. Do you know what this is, boy?"

"Name's Ned," I repeated. I looked down at the palm of his hand and saw a medium-sized shark's tooth from a sand shark. "Not bad," I said.

"But do you know what it is, boy?" he asked.

I could tell that it wasn't the kind of question where a person is looking for an answer; it was the kind of question where a person just wants you to look interested long enough so that he can get on with telling you the answer. I decided that I wouldn't play it that way even if he was a customer. Three *boys* in a row made me mean, so I said, "Medium-sized sand."

"What's that?" he shouted, cupping his hand over his ear again.

"Medium-sized sand," I repeated louder.

"That's a shark's tooth," he said, clamping his hand shut.

Shoot! I knew that it was a shark's tooth. I was telling him what *kind* it was and what size it was.

"That is a fossilized shark's tooth, boy," he said. "Found it just across the street."

"Name's Ned," I told him, and I walked away.

Sharks' teeth wash up all the time at the beach just across the road from Hixon's Landing. There's a giant fossil bed out in the ocean somewheres, and a vent from it leads right onto our beach. When the undertow gets to digging up out of that fossil bed and the tide is coming in, all kinds of interesting things wash in. Besides the sharks' teeth, there are also pieces of bones that wash up. I collect the backbones, the vertebraes, they're called; they have a hole in them where the spinal column went through. I have a whole string of them fixed according to size.

I collect sharks' teeth, too. I have been doing it for years. Mom started me doing it. It was Mom who made a study of them and found what kind of animal they might come from. Mom has these thorough ways about her. Dad says that Mom is smarter'n a briar and prettier'n a movie star.

Mom fixes the sharks' teeth that we collect into patterns and fastens them down onto a velvet mat and gets them framed into a shadowbox frame. She sells them down at the gift shop in town. And the gift shop isn't any tacky old gift shop full of smelly candles and ashtrays with the name of our town stamped on it. It's more like an art gallery. Matter of fact, it is called *The Artists' Gallery*, and Mom is something of an artist at how she makes those sharks' teeth designs. Some of the really pretty sharks' teeth Mom sells to a jeweler who sets them in gold for pendants. When she gets two pretty ones that match, he makes them into earrings.

When I find her a really special or unusual one, Mom says to me, "Looks like we got a trophy, Ned." When we get us a trophy, one that needs investigating or one that is just downright super special, we don't sell it. Shoot! We don't even think about selling it. There's nothing that bit of money could buy that we'd want more than having that there trophy.

Most everyone who comes to Hixon's Landing knows about Mom and me being something of authorities on fossils, especially sharks' teeth, so I figured that this old dude would either go away and not come back or hang around long enough to find out. Either way, I figured that I didn't need to advertise for myself and my mom.

The next day after school there was the old fellow again. I wouldn't want to sound braggy or anything, but I could tell that he was standing there at the end of our dock waiting for me to come home from school.

"Hi," I said.

"Well, boy," he said, "did you have a good day at school?"

"Fair," I answered. I decided to let the *boy* ride. I figured that he couldn't hear or couldn't remember or both. "Catch anything?" I asked.

"No, not today," he said. "Matter of fact I was just about to close up shop." Then he began reeling in, looking back over his shoulder to see if I was still hanging around. He didn't even bother taking the hook off his line; he just dumped rod and reel down on the dock and stuck out his hand to me and said, "Well, son, you can call me President Bob."

"What are you president of?" I asked.

"President of a college, upstate Michigan. But I'm retired now."

"Then you're not a president," I said.

"Not at the moment, but the title stays. The way that people still call a retired governor, *Governor*. You can call me President Bob instead of President Kennicott. Bob is more informal, but I wouldn't want you to call me just Bob. It doesn't seem respectful for a boy to call a senior citizen just Bob."

"And you can call me Ned," I said. "That's my name."

"All right, son," he said.

"After the first day, I don't answer to *son* or to *boy*," I said.

"What did you say your name was, son?"

Shoot! He had to learn. So I didn't answer.

"What is your name again?"

"Ned."

"Well, Ned, would you like to take a walk on the beach and hunt for some of those sharks' teeth?"

"Sure," I said.

He must have counted on my saying yes, because the next thing I see is him dropping his pants and showing me a pair of skinny white legs with milky blue veins sticking out from under a pair of bathing trunks.

As we walked the length of the dock, he told me that he was used to the company of young men since he had been president of a college. "Of course, the students were somewhat older," he said. Then he laughed a little, like punctuation. I didn't say anything. "And, of course, I didn't often see the students on a one-to-one basis." I didn't say anything. "I was president," he added. He glanced over at me, and I still didn't say anything. "I was president," he added.

"There's supposed to be some good fishing in Michigan," I said.

"Oh, yes! Yes, there is. Good fishing. Fine fishing. Sportsmen's fishing."

We crossed A1A and got down onto the beach from a path people had worn between the dunes, and I showed him how to look for sharks' teeth in the coquina. "There's nothing too much to learn," I said. "It's mostly training your eye."

He did what most beginners do, that is, he picked up a lot of wedge-shaped pieces of broken shell, mostly black, thinking they were fossil teeth. The tide was just starting on its way out, and that is the best time for finding sharks' teeth. He found about eight of them, and two of them were right nice sized. I found fourteen myself and three of mine were bigger than anything he collected. We compared, and I could tell that he was wishing he had mine, so I gave him one of my big ones. It wasn't a trophy or anything like that because I would never do that to Mom, that is, give away a trophy or a jewelry one.

President Bob was waiting for me the next day and the day after that one. By the time Friday afternoon came, President Bob gave up on trying to pretend that he was fishing. He'd just be there on the dock, waiting for me to take him sharks' tooth hunting.

"There's no magic to it," I told him. "You can go without me."

"That's all right, Ned," he said, "I don't mind waiting."

On Saturday I had a notion to sleep late and was in the process of doing just that when Mom shook me out of my sleep and told me that I had a visitor. It was President Bob, and there he was standing on his vanilla legs right by my bedroom door. He had gotten tired of waiting for me on the dock. It being Saturday, he had come early so's we could have more time together.

Mom invited him in to have breakfast with me, and while we ate, she brought out our trophy boxes. Our trophies were all sitting on cotton in special boxes like the ones you see butterflies fixed in inside a science museum. Mom explained about our very special fossils.

"Oh, yes," President Bob said. Then, "Oh, yes," again. Then after he'd seen all our trophies and had drunk a second cup of coffee, he said, "We had quite a fine reference library in my college. I am referring to the college of which I was president. Not my alma mater, the college I attended as a young man. We had quite a fine library, and I must confess I used it often, so I am not entirely unfamiliar with these things."

That's when I said, "Oh, yes," except that it came out, "Oh, yeah!" and that's when Mom swiped my foot under the table.

President Bob plunked his empty cup down on the table and said, "Well, come on now, Ned, time and tide wait for no man. Ha! Ha!"

I think that I've heard someone say that at least

four times a week. Everyone says it. Dad told me that it was a proverb, an old, old saying. And I can tell you that it got old even before I reached my second birthday.

When we got down to the beach, President Bob brought out a plastic bag and flung it open like a bag boy at the supermarket. But there wasn't much to fill it with that day because the currents had shifted and weren't churning up the fossil bed.

"I suppose you'll be going to church tomorrow," he said.

"Yes," I answered.

"I think I'll do some fishing in the morning. I'll probably have had enough of that by noon. I'll meet you at the dock about twelve-thirty. We can get started on our shark's tooth hunt then."

"Sorry," I said. "I help Mom with the sandwiches and then we clean things up and then we go to late services. Sunday is our busiest day."

"Of course it is," he said.

Mom and I got back about one-thirty and changed out of our good clothes before Dad came in as he always does on Sundays to grab some lunch before the men start coming back and he has to get busy with washing down motors and buying. (What he buys is fish from the men who have had a specially good run. Dad cleans them and sells them to markets back in town or to people who drive on out toward the beach of a Sunday. Sometimes, he gets so busy buying and cleaning that Mom and I pitch right in and give him a hand.)

Dad had not quite finished his sandwiches and had just lifted his beer when he got called out to the dock. There was this big haul of bass that some men were wanting to sell.

Mom and I were anxious to finish our lunch and clean up so's we could go on out and see if Dad would be needing some help when President Bob presented himself at the screen door to our kitchen.

"Knock, knock," he said, pressing his old face up against the screen. The minute we both looked up he opened the door without even an *if you please* and marched into our kitchen on his frosted icicle legs. "I think you're going to be interested in what I found today," he said. "Very interested."

Mom smiled her customer smile and said, "We are having very busy day, please to excuse if I continue with work."

"That's perfectly all right," President Bob said. "You're excused." Then he sat down at the table that Mom was wiping off. He held up the placemat and said, "Over here, Mama-san. You missed a spot."

Mom smiled her customer smile again and wiped the spot that he had pointed to, and President Bob put the placemat back down and emptied the contents of his plastic bag right on top of it. He leaned over the pile and using his forefinger began to comb through it. "Ah! here," he said. He picked up a small black thing between his thumb and forefinger and said to Mom, "Come here, Mama-san." *Mama-san* is some kind of Japanese for *mama*. A lot of people call my mom that, but she says it's okay because it is a term of respect, and a lot of people think that all Orientals are Japanese. Sometimes these same people call me Boy-san, which is to *boy* what Mama-san is to mama. They call me that because I have dark slanted eyes just like Mom's, except that hers are prettier.

"Look at this," President Bob said. "Look at it closely. I suspect that it is the upper palate of an extinct species of deep water fish."

Mom took it from his hand and looked at it and said, "Dolphin tooth." She put it back down and walked to the sink where she continued right on with washing up the dishes. She automatically handed me a towel to dry.

President Bob studied the dolphin's tooth and said to Mom, "Are you sure?"

She smiled and nodded.

"Quite sure?"

She nodded.

He asked once more, and she nodded again. Then he began poking through his collection again and came up with another piece. He beckoned to Mom to look at it closer, and she dried her hands and did that.

"Shell," she said.

"Oh, I beg to differ with you," he said.

"Shell," Mom said, looking down at it, not bothering to pick it up.

"Are you sure?"

She nodded.

"Quite sure?"

She nodded again, and I came over and picked it up off the table and held it up and broke it in two. I thought that President Bob was going to arrest me. "A piece of fossil that thick wouldn't break that easy. It's a sure test," I said.

"There are fragile fossils, I'm sure," President Bob said.

"I suppose so," I said. "But that shell ain't fossilized. Piece of fossil that thick wouldn't ever break that easy." I could see that you had to repeat yourself with President Bob. "That shell ain't fossilized."

"*Ain't* is considered very bad manners up North," President Bob said.

Shoot! *Bad manners* are considered bad manners down South, I thought. But I didn't say anything. President Bob kept sorting through his bag of stuff, studying on it so hard that his eyes winched up and made his bottom jaw drop open.

Mom finished washing the dishes, and I finished drying, and we asked if we could be excused, and

President Bob told us (in our own kitchen, mind) that it was perfectly all right, but would we please fetch him a glass of ice water before we left. We fetched it. He said, "Thank you. You may go now." I suppose that up North it's good manners to give people orders in their own house if you do it with *please* and *thank you* and no *ain'ts*.

It rained on Monday and it rained again on Tuesday, so I didn't see President Bob again until Wednesday after school. He was waiting for me at the end of the dock with his plastic sandwich bag already partly full. "Well," he said, "I guess I got a bit of a head start on you today."

I looked close at his bag and saw that he had a couple of nice ones—not trophies—but nice.

"I have homework," I said. "I can't walk the beaches with you today."

"What subject?"

"Math."

"Maybe I can help you. Did I tell you that I was president of a college."

"Really?" I said in my fakiest voice. "I think I better do my homework by myself."

"I'll wait for you," he said. "I promise I won't hunt for anything until you come back out."

"It'll probably take me the rest of daylight to do it," I said.

"Math must be hard for you," he said. "Always

was my strongest subject."

"It's not hard for me," I lied. "I just have a lot of it."

"Let me show you what I found today," he said.

"I don't think I have the time."

"Just take a minute."

Before I could give him another polite no, he had spread the contents of his bag over the railing of the dock. I looked things over real good. I knew he was watching me, so I wouldn't let my eyes pause too long on any one thing in particular. "Very nice," I said. "I've got to go now."

As I turned to walk back to our house, he called, "See you tomorrow."

The next day I didn't even walk to the dock. Instead I walked around to the side door of our house and threw my books on the wicker sofa on the screened porch and went up to my room and changed into my cut-offs. I had a plan; I was going to go back out the side door and walk a bit to the north before crossing the highway and climbing over the dunes onto the beach. I knew a place where a sandbar often formed, and Mom and I sometimes went there. When I was little, she'd put me in the sloop behind the sandbar, like at a wading pool at a regular Holiday Inn. As I got older, we'd go there on lazy days and take a picnic lunch and sift through the coquina of the sandbar. We've found about four trophies there. Not about, exactly four. Of the four, the first one was the most fun because it was the one we found by accident.

I felt if I could get out of the house and head north, I could escape President Bob and dig up some trophies that would make him flip.

But I didn't escape. When I came downstairs after changing my clothes, there he was sitting on the wicker sofa, his blueberry ripple legs crossed in front of him. He was leafing through my math book.

I told him hello.

He smiled at me. "Yes, yes, yes," he said, "I know exactly how it is to have to sit in school all day and have to hold your water. I am quite used to the habits of young men. I was president of a liberal arts college in Michigan." He noticed that I was wearing my cut-offs, my usual beachcombing outfit, so he slapped his thighs and set them to shimmying like two pots of vanilla yogurt. "I see you're ready. Let's get going. The tide's halfway out already, and as they say, 'Time and tide wait for no man.' Tide was better a few hours ago. I found a couple of real beauties. Locked them in the glove compartment of my car."

I walked with him to the beach, and we began our hunt. He wasn't bending over for falsies very much any more. Each time he bent over, he yelled, "Got one!" and then he'd hold it up in the air and wouldn't put it in his bag until I nodded or said something or both. President Bob ended up with about twenty teeth, one vertebra bone, and of the twenty, one was a real trophy, an inch long, heavy root and the whole edge serrated with nothing worn away. A real trophy.

I found eight. Three of them were medium, four of them were itty-bitty and one had the tip crushed off.

I got up early the next day and checked the tide; it was just starting out. Good, I thought. I crossed the road and ran out onto the beach, rolling up my pajama bottoms as I walked along. The tide was just right; it was leaving long saw-tooth edges of coquina, and I managed to collect eight decent-sized teeth and one right-good-sized one before I ran back home and hosed off my feet and got dressed for school. I stuffed my collection into the pockets of my cut-offs. I had to skip breakfast, a fact that didn't particularly annoy me until about eleven o'clock. That afternoon, for every two times President Bob stooped down and yelled, "Got one!" I did it three times.

On Friday I didn't want to skip breakfast again, and my mother for sure didn't want me to, so President Bob was way ahead.

On Saturday I got up before dawn and dressed and sat on our dock until I saw the first thin line of dawn.

Dawn coming over the intracoastal is like watching someone draw up a Venetian blind. On a clear day the sky lifts slowly and evenly, and it makes a guy feel more than okay to see it happen. But on that Saturday, I sat on the dock just long enough to make sure that daylight was to the east of me before I crossed the highway and began heading north. Shoot! I think that if the Lord had done some skywriting that morning, I wouldn't have taken the time to read it, even if it was in English.

Finally, I climbed to the top of a tall dune and walked up one and down another. I was heading for a place between the dunes about a mile to the north. I knew that during spring, when the moon was new, there was a tidewater between two of the dunes. Sharks' teeth got trapped in it, and sometimes Mom and I would go there if there was a special size she was looking for to finish an arrangement. You had to dig down into the coquina, and it wasn't much fun finding sharks' teeth this way instead of sauntering along the beach and happening to find them. But sometimes it was necessary.

I dug.

I dug and I dug and I dug.

I put all my findings into a clam shell that I found, and I dug, and I dug, and I dug. I felt the sun hot on my back, and I still dug. I had my back to the ocean and my face to the ground and for all I knew there was no sky and no sea and no sand and no colors. There was nothing, nothing and nothing except black, and that black was the black of fossil teeth.

I had filled the clam shell before I stopped digging. I sorted the teeth and put the best ones—there were fourteen of them—in my right side pocket—the one with a button—and I put all the smaller ones in my back pocket and started back toward home, walking along the strand. I figured that I had a good head start on the day and on President Bob. I would pepper my regular findings with the ones I had just dug up. I'd mix the little ones in with the fourteen big ones. But, I decided, smiling to myself, I'd have a run of about eight big ones in a row just to see what he would do.

My back felt that it was near to burning up, and I looked toward the ocean, and it looked powerful good. The morning ocean in the spring can be as blue as the phony color they paint it on a geography book map. Sometimes there are dark patches in it, and the gulls sweep down on top of the dark spots. I decided that I needed to take a dip in that ocean. I half expected a cloud of steam to rise up off my back. I forgot about time and tide and sharks' teeth and ducked under the waves and licked the salt off my lips as I came back up.

I was feeling pretty good, ready to face President

Bob and the world, and then I checked my pockets and found that about half the supply from my back pocket had tumbled out, and I had lost two big ones. I was pretty upset about that, so I slowed down on my walk back home. I crouched down and picked up shell pieces, something I thought that I had outgrown, but that is about how anxious I was not to let anything get by me. I found a couple of medium-sized ones and put them in my back pocket and began a more normal walk when my trained eye saw a small tooth right at the tide line.

I reached down to pick it up, figuring that, if nothing else, it would add bulk to my collection the way they add cereal to hot dog meat. I didn't have any idea how many baby teeth I had lost out of my back pocket.

When I reached down to pick up that little tooth, it didn't come up immediately, and I began to think that maybe it was the tip of a really big one. I stooped down and carefully scraped away the wet sand and saw that there were several teeth together. The tide was rushing back up to where I was, so I laid my hand flat down on the ground and shoveled up a whole fistful of wet, cool sand.

I walked back to the dune and gently scraped away the sand with the forefinger of my other hand, and then I saw what I had.

There were several teeth, and they were attached to a piece of bone, a piece of jaw bone. There was a space between the third tooth and the fourth, and the smallest tooth, the one on the end that I had first seen, was attached to the jaw bone by only a thin edge.

I had never seen such a trophy. I felt that the spirit of the Lord had come mightily upon me, like Samson. Except that I had the jawbone of a shark and not the jawbone of an ass. And I wanted to smite only one president, not a thousand Philistines.

I didn't run the rest of the way home. I was too careful for that. I walked, holding that trophy in my hand, making certain that it didn't dry out before I could see if the weak tooth was fossilized onto the bone.

I called to Mom when I came into the house and when she appeared at the door to the screened porch, I uncurled my fingers one by one until the whole bone and all four of the teeth were showing. I watched Mom's face, and it was like watching the dawn I had missed.

"Ah, Ned," she said, "it is the Nobel Prize of trophies." We walked into the kitchen. She wet a good wad of paper towels and lifted the jawbone carefully from my hand and put it down on that pad of paper. And then we sat down at the kitchen table and I told her about how I found it, and I told it all to her in detail. Dad came in and Mom asked me to tell him, and I did and she listened just as hard the second time.

We ate our breakfast, and afterwards, we wet the paper towels again and moved the trophy onto a plastic placemat on the kitchen table. Mom looked at it through the magnifying glass and then handed me the glass so that I could look at it, too.

While we were studying it hard like that, President Bob came to the screen door and said, "Knock, knock."

Mom nodded at me, her way of letting me know that I was supposed to invite him on in.

"Well, well," he said. "Are we ready for today's treasure hunt?"

"I guess so," I said, as easy as you please, moving a little to the left so that he could catch a glimpse of what Mom and I were looking at.

He gave it a glance and then another one right quick.

Mom and I looked at each other as he came closer and closer to the table. He studied that trophy from his full height and from behind a chair. Next thing, he moved in front of the chair. And next after that he sat down in the chair. And then, not taking his eyes off that trophy, he held his hand out for the magnifying glass and Mom took it from me and gave it to him.

The whole time he did this, I watched his face. His

eyes squinched up and his jaw dropped open and his nostrils flared. It was like watching a mini-movie called *Jealousy and Greed*.

I could feel myself smiling. "Found it this morning," I said.

Then I didn't say anything anymore. And I stopped smiling.

I thought about his face, and that made me think about mine. If his face was a movie called *Jealousy and Greed*, I didn't like the words I could put to mine.

I gently pushed the placemat closer to President Bob. "Look at it," I said. "Look at it good." I waited until his eyes were level with mine. "It's for you," I said. "It's a present from me."

"Why, thank you, boy," he said.

"Name's Ned," I answered, as I walked around to the other side of the table and emptied my pockets. "Do you think we can make something pretty out of these?" I asked Mom.

She gave me a Nobel Prize of a smile for an answer. President Bob didn't even notice, he was so busy examining the jawbone with which he had been smitten.

The Catchee

by Avery

When I was six years old, my brother Orville was twelve. Orville was a schoolboy patrol. He wore a day-glo red hat and a day-glo red strap that zagged across his chest and carried a pole with a day-glo red flag at the end of it. There was probably nothing doing at school that Orville enjoyed more than schoolboy patrolling. He would stand at the corner and wait for the light to change, and when it did, he would walk out into the street and hold out the pole until everyone who should have crossed the street had. That was his duty. I would stand on the curb and wait for him. That was my duty. My mother had put Orville in charge of my transportation to and from school. Our transportation then was walking, and I wasn't allowed to cross the street without him.

Sometimes Orville stood on the corner long after

everyone had emptied from the school building, and he'd walk home with me and with his pole with the day-glo red flag on the end of it. He'd walk over to the big industrial park that was growing up behind where we lived. Orville would pick a building and direct the people coming out.

There were no red lights in the industrial park. There were signs that had eight sides and some that had three. Orville would line up with one of the eight siders, and he'd lower his pole with the day-glo red flag at the end of it and allow people to cross the street in front of him. They'd come out like popcorn: nothing for a long time, then one and two at a time and then they'd come out a whole hopperful at a time. Most of the people coming out of the office buildings were girls. A lot of them smiled at Orville, and next to schoolboy patrolling, Orville liked those smiles best. He was twelve; he had begun liking girls when he was eleven. I would stand on the curb and wait for Orville.

Orville had tried most of the buildings in the industrial park. Remington became his favorite, and he always went back to it.

One day Orville was waiting outside the Remington. There was a little breeze that day, and that was another thing Orville liked a lot because the breezes would blow the girls' skirts up, and when I asked

Orville why he enjoyed that so much, he answered that he could see Schenectady. I didn't understand what he meant then, when Orville was already twelve, and I was still six.

Orville was at the best part of his patrolling that day, the part where the girls came out in twoses and threeses, that being the part where he got the most smiles, when he told me that he had to go to the bathroom. I was surprised. Because Orville didn't usually have to do ordinary things at inconvenient times. He told me to step off the curb and hold the pole with the day-glo red flag while he visited the bathroom in the Remington.

"You can't go in there," I said.

"Well, I sure can't go out here," he answered.

So Orville marched into the Remington, and for the first time I stood off the curb all by myself. I held the pole across the street, and the cars stopped, and the people crossed. I began to see why Orville enjoyed schoolboy patrolling so much. I was enjoying it pretty much myself. Although it didn't matter to me whether it was boys crossing or girls.

I had raised the pole once and let it down again when I felt someone tap me on my shoulder. I thought Orville was finished and wanted me to give him back his pole. I wouldn't turn around. I felt the poke on my shoulder again. I lowered the pole and stiffened my shoulders. "Listen," I snarled, "I'll give it back to you after the next batch crosses."

A voice, a voice that wore a uniform, answered, "Don't you know that it's illegal to impersonate a traffic officer?"

I turned around and saw that not only the voice but also the man who owned it wore a uniform. He took the pole with the day-glo red flag from me and, with his arm over my shoulder, walked me and the pole to the exit of the industrial park. As he guided me out, he told me how lucky I was that none of the cars had chosen to ride right through my flag. I could have gotten run over, standing off the curb like that, he said. In between everything else he said was the message: Don't do it any more. Ever. Again.

I waited for Orville on the sidewalk just outside the industrial park. Orville wasn't long in coming. He had gone to the bathroom just before the policeman came, and he finished just after the policeman took me with him.

While I waited, I figured out my life. I realized that the world is made up of two kinds of people: the catchers and the catchees. I was a catchee.

The next time it happened was a week later or maybe a month. When you can't tell time, it's hard to measure it. I was still in the first grade, and I had not yet learned all the short vowel sounds. It was after school, and Orville had given me money for a limeade from the Minute Market on the corner on the same side of the street as the school. Orville was schoolboy patrolling and doing it and doing it. I finished the limeade and slurped all the ice from the bottom. I held onto the paper cup for three red lights' worth of crossings after that, and the cup began to get mushy. I walked back to the corner where the Minute Market was, and I put the empty limeade in a container. The next thing I knew, I was being dragged by the back of my collar to the principal's office. The sixth grade teacher, Miss Elkins, was dragging me. She was also yelling at me, telling me that I had committed a federal offense. It wasn't until I got to the principal's office that I learned that I had mailed the lime cup. What I had thought had said *litters* had said *letters*. I explained to the principal that I didn't think that it was a federal offense to be only halfway through the short vowel sounds. The principal agreed, and Miss Elkins, realizing that it wasn't my fault that I was only halfway, agreed, too. But she wasn't too happy about it. She said that her birthday card to someone special was probably blurred to where it couldn't be delivered. She looked sideways at the principal when she said "someone special."

Orville was waiting for me when I came out of the principal's office. That was the first time he had had to wait for me instead of vice versa.

"What kept you, Avery?" he asked.

"I put a lime cup through the United States Mail," I said. Then I explained to him what had happened.

Miss Elkins was Orville's teacher then. He put his arm around my shoulder as we began to walk home and he said, "You know, Avery, if Miss Elkins were walking out of the Remington and a breeze blew her skirts way up past Schenectady, I wouldn't bother to look past New Rochelle."

There was only one spot where Orville's arm touched my shoulder that afternoon, and it was there for only three blocks and that was many years ago, but to this day I could still point to exactly where it was.

By the time I got into Miss Elkin's sixth grade myself, the industrial park had bulldozed its way over our old neighborhood of small houses. With the money my folks got for selling our old house, they had bought a new one. Not exactly new. It was middle-aged. It was also middle-sized, and the middle house on the block. We were now on the edge of rows of bigger houses. We knew there wouldn't be an industrial park moving up on us again because behind us was the old Talmadge estate that had been sold to developers. They were building houses on it. The new houses got bigger and bigger, row after row, the farther back from us you went. On the river row, they were as big as motels and had about that many bathrooms.

I was a schoolboy patrol in the sixth grade, but we were bused. We never took our flag poles home. They still had day-glo red, but they were locked up every night. Schoolboy patrolling wasn't what it had been when Orville had been it. And now it was called *school patrol*, not *schoolboy patrol*, because girls did it, too.

Orville had moved on to high school. All the girls that he had discovered now discovered him. He divided his spare time between talking on the telephone and working as a bag boy at the A & P. He never put his arm around my shoulder, and he made jokes all the time, out of everything.

I had managed to live a pretty normal life for a catchee. I had learned that the teacher would call on me for the *other* math problem, the one I had not done. In the fourth grade I was the only kid in my class who got lice, athlete's foot and poison ivy. I was probably the only kid in history who got them all at the same time. The only parts of me that didn't itch were my fingernails and, every now and then, the roof of my mouth.

"Cooties, crud, and creeping eruption," Orville said. He did a little shuffle with his feet and snapped his fingers to give it rhythm. I didn't think Orville was funny.

By the sixth grade I had learned that when they let people through seven at a time, I would be eighth. And that in the supermarket I would get the one cart out of seventy-five that had a stuck left rear wheel. And in the sixth grade I resumed my career as a police catchee.

After we moved, I had a lot of odd jobs. Some of my steady lawn mowing customers were hand-me-downs from Orville. He had to give them up to become a bag boy because there wasn't enough daylight when he got home. A lot of my piece work was for people who lived in the big houses along the river. I would feed and care for their parakeets when they went out of town. I would walk and brush their dogs; a lot of miniature poodles live in big houses. I was also hired to keep wild bird seed in the feeder and water in the bird bath. But the worst job I had was baby sitting with some azaleas.

Mrs. Wilkie had hired me. Mrs. Wilkie was a very worried lady who was going to Europe for three weeks. She was worried that her infant azaleas would die. Her house was so new that all the wall space around the light switches was spotless and the air inside it smelled fresh-sawed. And it was so big that if you put up a sign that said EMERGENCY, it could be mistaken for a hospital.

There were so many new houses in the neighborhood that things that should automatically go on were going off. Even on our edge, where the houses weren't as big as hospitals, we had our convenience problems: water for one thing and electricity for another. When it got very hot outside, and the air conditioners were set to switch on, they didn't. The power was so low that there wasn't enough of it in the wires to throw the switches. Walk past any box of circuit breakers at suppertime, and you could hear them moaning.

It sometimes took so long to fill the tub for a bath that you could turn the faucet on full force and go draw a map of the entire United States, marking the state capitals, Schenectady and New Rochelle, five major rivers, and still have the tub only half-full when you were finished. My mother was so pleased with her new-to-us middle-aged house that she never complained about its modern inconveniences or about having to wait until midnight to have enough water pressure to wash the dishes.

The first Saturday that Mrs. Wilkie was gone, I wandered over to her house to water. It was hot September. The electricity had been quaking in our house all day. When I got to the Wilkies', I saw that there was no garden hose outside. I walked around back and didn't find one there either. It would be a hot walk back to our house to get ours. I saw her sliding glass doors leading to her bedroom, and with just a little extra tug—about what you'd give to a lawn mower going uphill—I could open them. I figured that I would go through the house to her garage and get the hose. I never thought of it as breaking in.

I was halfway across the living room when the alarm went off. If you've never been inside an empty house with a burglar alarm going off inside it, I can only tell you that your head feels like a giant sinus cavity with an air raid alert inside.

I ran over to the entrance hall and threw every switch within sight, but the alarm wouldn't quit. Then I went into the hall closet and found the box of circuit breakers and threw every one there. The house went quiet. Everything suddenly sounded so hushed that I felt it necessary to tiptoe into the garage.

While I was in the garage, trying to uncoil one hundred and fifty feet of green garden hose from one hundred and twenty-five feet of black garden hose, I heard a voice come over the loud speaker, "All right, come on out." I paid no attention. I went on with my work. The voice came again. Closer and louder, and in uniform this time. "All right, come on out: we've got the house surrounded."

I realized they wanted me. So I came out. My hands were up from lifting the garage door, and the policemen told me to keep them exactly that way.

I walked down the driveway to the waiting police car. Mrs. Wilkie's neighbors saw me and said, "Why, it's Avery Basford." The cops asked if I would mind telling them what I was doing in there. I told them that I wouldn't mind telling them, and I didn't. But it took me thirty-five minutes to do it.

It seems that Mrs. Wilkie had been as worried about her house as she had been about her azaleas. She had asked her neighbors to listen for the alarm and to call the police if they heard it go off. Now, ordinarily, the minute that I pushed on the sliding glass door, the alarm would have gone off, and the neighbors would have found me outside, and ordinarily I could have explained to them. Ordinarily, I would never have been trapped inside. Ordinarily, Mrs. Wilkie's neighbors would not have reasoned that only a professional burglar would know how to enter a house and shut off an alarm. Ordinarily.

Ordinarily.

If everything had happened ordinarily, I would have found some other way to get trapped. For I was a catchee.

I became a police catchee again a little later that year, and it happened because of my Christmas spirit.

My mother was not only pleased with our new house, she was also proud of it. She hardly believed me when I told her that our whole house would fit inside the Wilkies' living room and dining room. "Bigger," she said, "isn't necessarily prettier." To her, there was nothing prettier in this whole world than our middle-sized picture window with our big Christmas tree just behind it.

She invited the ladies from our old neighborhood over for a party. Everyone from our old neighborhood had scattered to different middle-sized houses. She called it a class reunion.

"What class?" I asked.

"Low-income class," she answered.

I arrived home from school just as the ladies were opening the gifts that they were exchanging with each other. Sister Arnetta gave my mother a pair of underpants. My mother wouldn't stop raving about them. She called them panties, not underpants, and she said they were precious. She said that the only thing that Sister Arnetta could have done nicer would have been to give her a pair in each color of the rainbow.

That solved my problem about what to get my mother for Christmas.

I went to her room that night and I took the underpants from the box they came in. The box was from Eaton's, so I supposed that the panties were too. I put them in a plain brown paper bag from the grocery store, and I layered the bag between my math and social studies books. I decided that I would go to town straight from school and buy my mother those same precious panties in as many colors of the rainbow as I could afford.

I found Eaton's department of underwear with no trouble at all, but I had not counted on how pastel it would be. In my black skin, blue jeans and maroon sweater, I felt like a walking exclamation point in a sea of whispers.

No one took my being there seriously. No one asked, "May I help you?" So I tried to help myself. I pulled a corner of the precious panties from the plain brown paper bag, and I tried to match them with the assortment that was on top of the counter. But I couldn't tell if they were the precious kind or some other. All the materials looked alike, and they were all basically the same shape. I needed to see the label for size and variety.

The label on women's underpants is on the inside. I figured that if I could get a hold on it, I could let it poke out of the bag. Then I would only have to match numbers. I reached into the bag to let my fingers do the walking and was gazing over the counter and up at the ceiling as I concentrated on the touch system inside the bag.

I felt a tap on my shoulder.

The tap wore a uniform. So did the voice. "Better come along with me, sonny."

I turned around and saw a store security guard.

"What's the mater?" I asked.

"Where did you get those panties?" he asked looking at the bag.

"From my mother," I answered.

"Did she give them to you as an advance Christmas present?" His tone was sarcastic.

"These panties are not mine," I said.

"Oh, I believe that they're not yours. But it's your job to convince me that they're your mother's. Just show them to me, and if they've been worn, you won't have to say one more thing to me."

"They're brand new."

The guard smiled. "That's what I thought. Can you show me a receipt?"

"No. They were a gift. People never put receipts in with gifts."

"They never put them in with stolen goods either. Suppose you come along with me, sonny."

I knew it would get down to that.

He took me to an office where some manager sat behind a desk. "I found this young fellow shoplifting in ladies' bloomers." he said.

"No, you didn't." I explained quietly. "You only caught me feeling them."

The two men exchanged looks. "I brought these panties from home. *Bloomers*, if you want to call them that."

"To whom do you say they belong?" the manager asked.

"To my mother."

"Suppose we call her and check it out."

"Oh, please don't do that. She won't be at all surprised."

"You mean that you've been in trouble before?"

I could see that anything I said would be used against me. That was one of the problems of being a catchee. "Look," I said, "call my big brother Orville. He works at the A & P." I looked at my watch. "He gets the car on Wednesdays because he brings the groceries home. If you get hold of him now, he'll stop here on his way home and straighten everything out."

I was left in the manager's outer office in my own custody until Orville came. We got it all straightened out. And the manager even walked us over to the department of underwear and introduced us to a saleslady who wore a badge saying MISS HINKEL. Miss Hinkel helped me find the underpants. I could afford one pink and one pale blue so I paid for them, and we left.

As we were driving home, I said to Orville, "You know, Orville, this never would have happened if I weren't a catchee. I've been a catchee all my life."

Orville understood what I meant by catchee because he had noticed it about me. Orville said that he had thought about it, and he thought, too, that it was time to talk to me about it.

"Avery," he said, "being a catchee can make you two things. It can make you very honest."

"I believe that, brother. I can see that. I don't stand a chance being anything but honest."

"And," Orville added taking a hand from the steering wheel to pat my knee, "it can make you very brave."

"How can it do that?" I asked.

"Well, Ave," he said, "it can make you brave this way. Most guys never know whether or not they're going to get caught. They just never know, and they live in fear of it. But you—you being a catchee—never have to worry about *whether*. You just don't know when. Don't you see, Ave? You are never afraid because you are always prepared for the worst. Like when the guy in the department store fingered you. You stayed calm. You didn't lose your temper. You didn't go crying to Momma and give your surprise away. You stayed cool. You are free of fear. And that, Avery, makes a guy very brave. Honest and brave. That's a great combination. I think you're going to be a leader of men, brother."

I liked what Orville said. A clarinet began playing inside me. I didn't even tell Orville thank you. I sat there holding that box of panties, pink and pale blue,

Christmas wrapped, and the white ones in the plain brown bag. I sat there and listened to that clarinet; it was playing "honest and brave" inside me.

We came to the intersection of Heavener and Forsythe, and Orville drove right through a yellow light, yellow making it to red before we were all the way across.

Orville looked over at me. We smiled at each other. Both of us were glad that it wasn't me driving.

In
the Village
of the
Weavers

by Ampara

I am Ampara, and it is I who will tell to you the story of Antonio and me. Antonio speaks in two languages, the language of Quechua and that of Spanish. I also speak in two languages, Spanish and English. Spanish is the first language for both Antonio and me, but it is English that you and I have between us, and that is why I must tell the story.

I am a guide. I guide the tours of the people like yourself, who come from the United States to my country to visit. My country is Ecuador on the continent of South America. The story of Antonio and me begins when I was in the final stages of training to become a guide. That was one year and a half before now.

A person in the final stages of training is called *la novicia*, what you in English would call an apprentice. It is the duty of the apprentice in the final stages of learning to take the tours with a finished guide and to listen and to watch what the guide does. But it is not the duty of the apprentice to do anything or to say anything; it is her duty only to learn.

On my first day of the final training we picked up our tourists from the hotel in Quito, which is the capital of my country. The tourists boarded the bus, and the guide counted them. It is necessary to count the tourists after each time the bus stops because the guide is responsible for returning to the hotel all the people who started out.

We then drove on the Pan American Highway through our beautiful Andes Mountains. As we did so, the guide pointed out things of interest in our country and things of beauty in our countryside. She told the tourists the names of the mountains. Some of them have Indian names and some of them have Spanish names, for these are the two main languages of my country.

The guide stopped at a roadside stand and bought cherimoya fruit for the people of the United States to taste. The cherimoya fruit is also very wonderful to smell, and many of the tourists liked it very much and some did not like it at all, but all of them took pictures of the family that was selling the fruit by the roadside. I stood outside the bus, and I thought to myself that the air of our Andes Mountains is like a fruit, it is that natural and that ripe and that full of the sun. But I said nothing, for it is the duty of the apprentice guide to say nothing.

We next stopped at the mark of the Equator. My country of Ecuador is named for the Equator, which passes through it. Everyone got out at the monument to the Equator, and they took very many pictures. Sometimes the guide took the pictures for them. When everyone got back onto the bus, the guide once again counted the people.

The first village that we stopped at is called the village of Calteron. The people of this village make the bread dough figures. They are brightly colored and all are made by hand, and the tourists got out and bought very many of them to take back to the United States to hang on their Christmas trees. Perhaps, you have been to the house of someone who has some of these bread dough ornaments. They are very colorful and very humorous. The guide again counted the people when they got on the bus.

Next we stopped at a hacienda of the Otovalo people. The Otovalo are Indian people who speak the language of Quechua. The men wear the dark blue poncho and the white pants and wear their hair in a braid that hangs down their backs. The Otovalo women wear blouses which have beautiful and bright embroidery, and around their necks they wear many, many strings of beads.

This village is a village of weavers, and the first person who heard the motor of the bus as it drove into the small square ran to tell another. And the other told another and very soon everyone was telling everyone and even before the bus had opened its doors, all the people of the village were rolling straw mats onto the ground of the village square, and they spread their weavings on top of these mats.

What they weave is beautiful, really beautiful, to see. They weave small rugs and tapestries of wool. They use all the colors and all the shades of all the colors. Even the deep greens and the deep browns that they use in their weavings are as bright as when the Andes sun flashes on the dark bark of a tree. The designs are of fish and of birds and of the symbols of the ancient gods of the tribe of the Otovalo people.

On that day when I first went to the village of the weavers, I stood back and watched how the finished guide helped the people of the tour and the people of the village make business together. The men of the village are the weavers, and it is the men who sell the large weavings, the rugs and the wall hangings. The women and children sell the small things, the shawls and the pocketbooks.

But there was in that village on that day one child who was selling the large weavings. That child was a boy, and even in this village where all the children have straight black hair and dark brown eyes and where all the boys wear the white pants and the navy blue poncho, this boy stood out. His eyes danced like pieces of polished stone under the surface of a mountain lake.

The weavings that he had to sell were very beautiful to see. I was looking at them very much when this boy said to me, "Bonita, Senora," and he pointed to his weavings that he had spread over the ground. He was telling me that they were pretty. I could see that he wanted to make some business with me. Since I was not yet a guide, and I was not yet wearing the uniform of the guide, he thought that I was a tourist from the United States. I told him in Spanish that I was a tour guide, a *novicia*, and I hoped that he understood.

He did understand because he immediately turned his bright eyes from me and picked up the small rug that he had just pointed to and carried it to a lady who had come from the bus and who was carrying a very large pocketbook. It was very clear to me that this boy wanted to make business, not conversation.

This boy made me very curious and I followed him. I asked him his name, and without stopping to look back he answered, "Antonio."

The reason that he answered me at all was because he knew that it was important to be nice to tour guides so that they will bring the buses to his hacienda instead of to another one of weavers. I thought to myself that this was very smart of Antonio. The brightness that I had seen in his eyes came from a fine fire in his brain.

"How old are you?" I asked.

"*Doce,*" he answered.

The woman to whom he was showing the beautiful weaving shook her head and said, "No, no. Twelve is too much." (Many tourists from the United States have learned in Spanish the words for the numbers and for the restrooms.)

"Pardon, Madam," I said. "The boy was not saying the price; he was telling to me his age." Then I asked Antonio how much he was asking for the weaving, and he told me. I translated our *sucres* into dollars for the woman, and she bought it. Antonio looked very pleased. As he walked back to his place to get another weaving, I followed him and asked him why he was making business instead of his father.

"My grandfather has cut his foot, and he cannot run when the bus arrives," Antonio said. "He comes now."

I saw a man walking up the path. He was leaning on a cane. When he arrived to the place where we were, Antonio immediately handed to him the dollars he had received from the tourist woman.

"For the tapestry of fishes," Antonio said.

"Good," said the grandfather.

I looked down and saw the foot of the grandfather. It was cut very badly and was very ugly with pus. It was oozing all around the cut and the skin was stretched so thin from the swelling that I could see dark colors under the skin churning in the manner of the insides of an earthworm freshly turned up out of the ground. The foot itself was shapeless from swelling, and it was something ugly, really ugly to see.

I had to make myself very brave to look at his foot without becoming sick.

The grandfather noticed me studying his injury, and I became embarrassed that he should have seen me looking at his sore. "How long has it been like that?" I asked.

"Ten days ago he cut it," Antonio answered. "It is worse now than when it happened."

"It is infected," I said. "He should see a doctor."

The grandfather shook his head very hard, and he was shaking it in the direction of no.

"My grandfather does not like doctors," Antonio said.

"Then he must come with me on the bus. I will take him to the hospital in Quito. The nurse will fix his foot."

The grandfather forced himself to stand up to his full height, and the pain that caused to him was there to see in his eyes and in the turn of his mouth. When he stood thus, his face was level with mine, and he said to me, "If I go to the hospital, I will die, and I will hate you."

To hear him speak so was to cause in me a chill like sudden dusk in the thin air of the Andes. The grandfather was telling me that his spirit would hate me, and everyone in my country knows that it is dangerous to be hated by the spirits of the dead.

"Take me to your house," I said to Antonio.

Antonio looked to his grandfather, and the grandfather nodded yes. As we walked down the path to Antonio's house, I called to the tour guide that I would return before the bus would leave.

There was an old woman in the house. It was Antonio's grandmother. She spoke only Quechua, and what I told Antonio in Spanish, I had him translate into Quechua and tell to her. This is what I told Antonio, which I translate into English to tell to you: Boil some fresh well water. Soak two very clean and very white cotton towels in the boiling water and wring them out. Place the hot towels, as hot as the old man can stand, on the festering sore. Do that at least four times a day. After each time, the towels must be washed clean.

As Antonio explained it to the grandmother, the grandmother nodded again and again. As Antonio and I walked back to the village square, I said to him,

"You will do it to your grandfather as soon as the bus leaves." He answered that he would.

When we returned to the bus, the guide again counted the people and we went on our way to the next hacienda where everyone got out of the bus and had a very large, very late lunch.

I thought about Antonio and his grandfather a very long time. On the road back to Quito I decided that after we would let our passengers off at the hotel, I would myself go to the hospital and there I would ask what more I could do for the wound of the grandfather.

At the hospital they gave me two kinds of medicine. One kind was meant to be placed on the cut, right on it, and the other was meant to be swallowed. I put the last one away altogether because I knew that that grandfather would hate me if I asked him to take inside of himself white man's medicine.

On the following day we did the city tour, so it was not until the third day that our bus returned to the hacienda of Antonio.

"My grandfather waits for you," Antonio said to me.

"I will go by myself. I remember the way. You stay here and sell the tapestries."

The grandmother of Antonio was waiting by the door of their house, and she called to her husband when she saw me walking down the path. The grandfather came to the door and said, *"Buenos dias, senorita."*

They led me inside their house, and the grandfather sat down on a fresh straw mat. He took the clean towel that was covering his wound, and I looked once again at the meat of his foot. It was not worse, and the fact that it was now clean made it easier to be looked at.

I took the tube of salve that had been given to me by the doctor at the hospital and I opened it very slowly. I very gently squeezed the tube from the bottom and put some on the tip of the forefinger of my right hand. I held my finger out for the grandmother to see, and she nodded to me to show me that she understood. I gently rubbed the medicine over the open cut, right on the place where the injury was first made. I very carefully and very slowly fastened the cap back onto the tube. I held the tube in both my hands while I told the grandfather that now each time after the hot towels, he must rub on his foot some of this good medicine. I asked him to hold out his right hand, and he did so. I placed the tube in his hand and closed his fingers around it. You can see that I made a little ceremony with the tube of the medicine. I felt that it would be better that way.

When I returned to the village square, Antonio

was selling a small rug and he asked me with his eyes to stand by him which I did. After he finished his sale he asked me how I had found his grandfather, and I told him that I had given him some powerful medicine. Antonio nodded to show me that he understood.

I must tell you that every time our tour bus came to the hacienda, the grandfather, the grandmother and I had a meeting in the house, and I examined the wound. Each time, it got better and better, I am happy to tell you.

It was to happen that the first day that I wore the uniform of a finished guide was the day that Antonio's grandfather ran into the village square with all the other men when the sound of the bus motor was heard. I can tell you that I thought it was a good sign for my career as a finished guide.

After all the tourists had come down off the bus and were busy examining the weavings, I walked over to the grandfather and I asked him, "Where is Antonio?"

"He comes now with the pocketbooks," the grandfather answered.

I looked down the path and saw Antonio walking so slowly that his hemp sandals made dragging marks from backward to forward. I called to him, and he raised his head very slightly, but he continued to drag his feet from backward to forward.

He arrived in the village square and began to sell the pocketbooks and the shawls without telling me hello.

"Antonio!" I called to him. "Hey! Antonio, look. I am a full guide now."

"I see," he said.

"Thank you," I said.

"Grandfather is well now, and I am back to selling the pocketbooks," he said.

"Are you not happy that your grandfather can now run and do business when the bus arrives?"

"I am happy that Grandfather can run, but I was very able to do the business of the rugs and the large tapestries." He smoothed the shawls that he was carrying on his arms and then he said, "Now, senorita, I must find my way between all those silly children to make business."

I can tell you that I was mad as I have not been mad for a long, long time. It may be said that I have saved the leg of his grandfather, for surely, he would have lost his leg if the infection had not been stopped. It may be said that I saved only the foot, but surely for a foot a person can be thankful. I did not expect a large thank you. I wanted only a simple message with the eyes as the grandmother and the grandfather had given me. But Antonio had hardly even looked at me. I called out to him. "The words of *thank you* will not stick in your throat."

Antonio answered, "Everyone expects an orphan to be grateful."

"I did not know that you are an orphan," I answered.

Antonio appeared surprised that I had answered him so, but I did not give him a chance to say one thing more.

You are probably thinking that I was also mad that Antonio did not mention one word about my wearing the uniform of the guide. That is so. If I am very honest with you, the way I want to be, I have to admit that I would have liked it if Antonio had told me some congratulations on getting my uniform.

When I returned to the bus, I was very busy counting the people. The bus was already moving when I turned to pick up my microphone to make the announcement about our next stop for lunch. I saw a package on the seat where the tour guide sits. I knew that it was a gift from the grandfather of Antonio. I did not say anything, and I did not open it, for I did not want the people on the bus to think that I had been paid by the people of the village. In the United States such payments are called *kickbacks*, and they are thought of as Watergates, which no one in the United States likes.

I did not open the package until I returned to my house. The grandfather had made for me a tapestry with the design of Tumi, the god of medicine. He had made this Tumi look very happy. The color of the background was a blue, a deep, rich blue like the color of my uniform. There were no pale colors in it altogether, and it was something beautiful, really beautiful, to see.

I was next sent on a long tour to the Amazon part of our country, and that is why it happened that it was three weeks before I again was in charge of a tour to the village of Antonio and his grandfather.

As soon as I could make my way over to them, I did, and I said, "I enjoy very much to have a picture of Tumi." The three of us smiled at each other, and I wished that the grandmother was there, too, but I had no time to ask about her. It was a very active time for me, translating *sucres* into dollars. It was not until the doors of the bus were closed and we were driving along the Pan American Highway that I remembered to count the people. I counted the tops of the heads to myself, "*Uno, dos, tres . . . diez y seis.*" There were *sixteen* tops of head on the bus now and only *quince*, fifteen, when we had boarded in Quito. This had never before happened.

I saw under head number sixteen, way in the back of the bus where the tourists never like to sit, a pair of eyes as black as obsidian. My eyes and those eyes snapped together, and because my eyes lingered on the back of the bus, the tourists all turned around to see what it was that held my eyes. "That is Antonio,"

I said. "He will ride with us to our next stop which is lunch."

"How will he get back?" one tourist asked me.

"After we finish our lunch, our bus rides this way back and we leave him out on the highway, and he will walk down the road to his house." I made a quick survey of everyone on the bus, and I understood from their faces that except for one man and one woman, who were a couple traveling together, no one seemed to mind. I did not want to make anyone unhappy with the way I did the tours. Whereas all the other people on the bus seemed pleased to have Antonio with them on the bus and were asking him questions in English, which he did not understand, this couple did not even turn around to look at him. I translated the questions such as, "How old are you?" and "Where do you go to school?" into Spanish. But when they asked him what did his mother and his father do, I pretended that I did not hear the question over the rattle of the bus, and I said, "Antonio will sing some songs for you."

I didn't know if Antonio could sing, but I thought that if he could not carry a tune at all, I would blame it on the rumblings of the bus.

But Antonio did sing. He sat in his seat on the very back of the bus and sang one song, then two, then three, all of them in the Quechua language. The songs were lively songs, clear and bright, as if his notes had been made by the colors in the weaving of the god Tumi. When he finished, everyone clapped, even the couple who had not looked happy about Antonio.

Antonio waited with the driver while we ate. When he got out at the place on the Pan American Highway where there is the road that leads to his village, many people waved goodbye to him, and the couple who had caused me to worry took his picture with a camera.

The next time our tour bus stopped at the village of the weavers, there were ten children who wanted to ride the bus. I could see that Antonio had done some very good advertisements for himself. But my group this time was twenty-five, and I could not fit ten more on the bus even if they were children. Antonio himself solved the problem. He pointed to three girls and said to them, "Come!" He then turned to me and explained, "They know the Quechua songs."

When we got onto the bus, I told my group that the children from the village of the weavers would entertain them with some songs. And the children did, and the people on the bus liked it very much.

The following week Antonio and his singing group boarded the bus, and once again they were very popular. When the bus stopped on the highway to let them off, everyone moved to that side of the bus and waved goodbye many, many times. The tourists took many pictures of them, too, and Antonio liked that very much.

Antonio was never long without surprises for me. The third week when he boarded the bus, he carried with him many weavings both large and small." What is this now?" I asked.

"I decided that while you are at the luncheon hacienda, I can make some business with the other people from other tours who go there. The girls will sell the pocketbooks and the shawls. I will sell the rugs and tapestries."

I said nothing, for it seemed to me that Antonio had a very good idea in that.

The singing of the children riding the bus between the two haciendas became a feature of my tours. Antonio placed himself in charge of the singing, and it was Antonio who decided which of the children could ride the bus. My bus tours became famous, and my boss in Quito would say to the visitors from the United States, "Our best guide is Ampara. You will enjoy her tour."

There was one song that the children sang that I loved more than all the others. It was a song in Quechua, and I asked Antonio to teach it to me. Antonio told me no.

"Why no?" I asked him.

He answered me, "If I teach you that song, you will then sing it, and you will no longer ask me to ride the bus."

"I never asked you even the first time," I said.

"That is true," he answered. "But now I am very popular, and I sell many weavings at the hacienda of the resturant. I make good business, and it is not the business of pocketbooks and shawls; it is the business of the men."

I said nothing to Antonio, but I am here to tell you this in English—it is something that I learned from the tourists who ride my bus—I was pissed off with Antonio. I would have told him that he could not ride the bus at all any more, but I have already mentioned that my tours were now famous, partly because of Antonio. You might ask, why did I not dismiss Antonio and allow only the girls to ride the bus? You might say, weren't they also singing? But I would have to answer you that I felt a certain attachment to Antonio, and I had the feeling that if I dismissed him from the bus, it would only make him more of the way he was. I wanted to show him that it is good to be smart, but it is also good to do unnecessary things like putting a design on the border of a rug just to make it more beautiful. It is sometimes necessary to use unnecessary words like *thank you* and *please* just to make life prettier.

After we had been making the tours for several

months, I had heard the songs very often and I came to know all the words in Quechua, the words that I had asked Antonio to teach me. But about this I said nothing.

I was beginning to think that I had made a very bad mistake by not telling Antonio that I was pissed off with him, because as he and his singing group continued to ride the bus, he was becoming very swollen-headed and very bossy with the girls who rode with him. Part of the reason for this swollen-headedness was that many people asked to have their pictures taken with him to carry back to the United States for souvenirs. Antonio would arrange the girls in front of him, and he learned to say in English, "Cheese!" just before the picture was taken. Antonio loved best of all the Polaroid instant pictures that were in color.

Now I must tell you why I was glad that I held my tongue about the many things that made me mad at Antonio. It happened after I had been wearing the uniform of the finished guide for more than a year.

There came on my bus a man and his wife who were from Kansas in the United States. In Kansas in the United States there are no mountains and no ocean, and they loved everything about my country of Ecuador. And they had with them not only two cameras, one of which was the Polaroid kind, which I told you was loved by Antonio, but they had also with them a cassette recording machine. They occupied themselves with taking very many pictures of our Andes mountains and also with recording what I had to say into the microphone as I explained to them about our beautiful countryside.

As we were leaving the hacienda of the weavers, Antonio and his group began singing, and the man from Kansas gave to me the cassette and asked me to please make for him a recording of the children as they sang.

I went to the back of the bus and pointed the little microphone that was attached to the cassette machine toward the children. They had not before seen a cassette player, but they knew that it was special, and they sang very beautifully, and they smiled as they sang. They were in the middle of my favorite song when Antonio's voice cracked. His eyes looked up at me, and they were frightened. He tried once again to sing, but he could not. He could not control the sounds that came from him. His voice shot high when it should not have. I picked up the song and sang along with the girls until the song was altogether finished. Then I shut off the machine and took it back to the man from Kansas, who thanked me very much.

Then Antonio did an unexpected thing. He walked forward before the bus stopped and sat down next to me on the seat of the guide. "You know the Quechua song," he said.

"Yes," I answered. "I have known it now for many months."

"I do not know what happened to me today," Antonio said. "My voice is like a forest animal; it makes strange sounds from hidden places."

"It is the voice of your manhood that comes forth," I said to him.

"Yes," he said. "There will be a time now when I will not be able to sing."

"That is so."

"But I will continue to ride with you on the bus," he said. "My grandparents have come to depend upon the money from my earnings at the hacienda of the restaurant."

"You can continue to ride on the bus with me even if you do not sing."

"When the full voice of my manhood arrives, it will flow strong all the way to the front of the bus."

"Yes," I said. "I am sure the voice of your manhood will be loud."

"I did not say loud. I said strong."

"Strong?"

"Yes, strong," he said. "Loud was the voice of my childhood."

I laughed. "I do not believe that you will stop being loud."

"A stubborn voice is loud," he said. "A trusting

69

voice can speak softly and still be heard. My new voice will be deep, but it will be soft, and it will speak the language of Quechua, and that of Spanish," he said. Then he looked at me very long and said, "And English."

"But you do not speak English," I said.

"Not yet, but you will teach it to me," he said. "Please."

"Since when have you wanted to learn English?" I asked.

"For a long time. But I did not ask. I thought that if I asked you to teach me English, you would say that you would teach me only if I taught you the Quechua songs, and if I taught you those, I thought you would never again ask me to ride the bus."

"I would never think in that way, Antonio."

"I know now that you would not," he said. "I promise that I shall learn to speak English as Ampara speaks it." Then he hummed his Quechua song until his voice once again cracked, and he walked to the back of the bus laughing at himself.

And that is the story of Antonio and me. I told you that I must tell the story, for English is not yet within Antonio. But soon it will be, and then he will speak for himself, and his speech will be soft and polite, but firm. And I, Ampara, will feel proud that I was the guide who got him there.

At
The
Home

---

by Phillip

I won't bother you with details of how I broke my arm. Let me just say that some people are not as well coordinated on a skateboard as are some other people. I'll let it go at that. I might also add that you can break an arm from a skateboard even if you're not doing anything fancy on it. I wouldn't even bother to mention my broken arm at all except that it figures into the story that I have to tell, and my story is rather complicated, so I have to lay it all out. Maybe I should add one more little thing, except that it wasn't so little. Mine was not a simple break, what is called a simple fracture. Mine was a compound, a compound fracture, which means that the bone is broken in more than one place. Two, in my case. I'll let it go at that except for one more small matter. It was my left arm, not my right, and I am right-handed, so I had to go to school anyway.

At school I found out that a broken left arm, even if it is compound, is of interest to other kids only for as long as it takes them to autograph the cast. After that, they don't think about it long enough to offer to carry your books home for you. Not that I ever carried that many books home, anyway. I'll let it go at that, except for one more tiny thing I should mention about a compound fracture of the left arm. Skateboarding is out until the cast comes off. I suppose that a really well-coordinated person could learn to balance himself with one arm in a sling, but I've already mentioned that I am not in your basic category of the really well coordinated.

I came directly home from the school bus stop that Tuesday in April, the first day after I had broken my arm, and found my mother ready to go to the old folks' home. She goes there one afternoon a week and reads to some of the people. She also helps them make out checks or write letters. She usually stays until about five-thirty, when they are settled down for their evening meal. I had told my mother that I needed some batteries for my cassette player since I had decided to use this broken-arm time to improve my impersonations. Magic would have been my first choice, but I did mention that I am not terribly well coordinated. I'm not spastic or anything, but in order to do magic, the kind of coordination you need is beyond basic, beyond *very*, somewhere in the category of superb.

I asked my mother to take me to the discount store where I could buy some batteries for my cassette, and then I'd walk home. Unfortunately, I could not immediately find my cassette recorder, and I needed to find it because I couldn't remember the exact size of the batteries it needed. Who can remember whether something takes C or D? It had been a long time since I had practiced my impersonations. It was also a long time before I found my cassette recorder. I suppose that I was making my mother nervous because she kept asking me if I had looked here or looked there; and finally, she said that she was going out to the car to wait, and I told her that it was not so easy looking for something with only one arm, and she told me that the better part of looking for something was thinking about it, like when did you use it last, and I told her that I couldn't understand her hurry to get to the old folks' home because those people weren't going anywhere anyway, and she told me that she would wait for me in the car with the motor running and using up gasoline and for me to remember the energy shortage.

I found my cassette player in my bookcase behind the Hardy Boys. Its microphone cord was hanging down, and the first three times I looked at that cord

I thought it was a magic marker stain. Once I found it, I didn't hang around to take out the batteries. I rushed with it out to the car, where my mother was sitting not only with the motor running but also with the car door on the passenger's side open.

"I'm going straight to the home," she said. "You can go to the convenience store across the street from there and get your batteries. Then you can come over to the home and meet me, and I'll drive you back after I've finished with what I have to do."

"Batteries cost more at a convenience store," I said.

"Get them there anyway."

"At a convenience store they cost even more than they do at a regular store. Why don't you drop me off at the discount store?"

"For some reason, I seem to be running late today. I can't seem to find the time to make an extra stop."

"At a discount store, they only cost—"

"I'll pay the difference!"

"It will be a lot."

"I'll pay it."

"A whole lot."

"I'll pay it."

"It'll be more than the difference between a discount store and a regular store. What I mean by a *regular* store is like a camera shop, where it isn't self-service—"

"I'll pay it. It will be cheaper than driving miles

out of my way and using up all that gas," Mother muttered.

So I bought the batteries at the Minute Market across the street from the home. I kept the cash register receipt to help Mother keep her promise about paying the difference. I wandered into the lobby of the old folks' home. I sat there, trying to put the batteries in one-handedly, when this old man came up to me and said, "Need some help there, young man?"

He had an accent that sounded Communist. He took the cassette player from me and set the batteries in it just right, all the pluses where they ought to be and all the minuses where they belonged, too.

I had left an old cassette in it, and I wondered what was on it, so I turned the machine on and heard Walter Cronkite giving the evening news. I had worked on my Cronkite impersonation a long time before I decided that you can't make anything sound like a world crisis until your voice has changed.

The old man picked up the microphone, and I pushed down on the *record* button, and he began to sing. He sang a whole song all the way through in some foreign language, and I asked him what the language was.

"Ukrainian," he answered. I didn't say anything, because I didn't know what to say. I didn't know where Ukrainia was. He must have read my mind because he asked, "You know the Ukraine?"

I shrugged.

"It's part of Russia," he said. "What I sang was an old folk tune, something that is very appropriate, coming as it does from an old folk." Then he laughed at his little joke.

I laughed, too. I was glad that I had guessed right about his accent; Russia was Communist. I played back what he had sung, and he was so pleased with hearing it that he asked me to show him which buttons to push so that he could record another song. He learned about the buttons very quickly, and he sang not one but two more songs before my mother appeared.

"Ah!" the Ukrainian said, "so you are Leona's son." With his accent, the word *son* came out sounding like I was a whole generation, which I am because I am an only child.

That night after supper I picked up the cassette player. They had announced on TV that Rich Little would be on *Hollywood Squares*, and I thought that it would be very clever to impersonate an impersonator doing an impersonation, if you get what I mean.

I rewound my tape, and I happened to push the *play* button instead of *record*, and some of the Ukrainian folk songs came pouring out. I shut it off, getting ready to rewind again, when my father yelled, "Wait a minute!"

Needless to say, I waited.

"What's the matter?" I asked.

"Nothing's the matter. I would like to hear the rest of that."

So I played it to the end. My father asked me where I had recorded those tunes, and I told him. "Don't erase it," he said. "I'd like to have it."

"But I need the cassette. I don't have another one."

"Buy one," he said, and reached in his pocket and pulled out a five dollar bill and didn't say anything about giving him change.

I took the money and didn't make any suggestions. "Why do you want that tape?" I asked.

"I like those songs. My mother used to sing them to me. She came from the Ukraine. What did you say the old man's name is?" he asked.

"I didn't say. I don't know his name."

"Why don't you find out? Maybe Mother will know."

So I went to my mother and asked, "Do you know who is the person at the old folks' home who has gray hair and who isn't very tall and is a little bit stooped and speaks with an accent and wears a beige suit and walks with a cane?"

"Give me a real hint. Man or woman?"

"Man. I said *beige suit*."

"The women wear suits, mostly beige. Give me another hint."

"He was very old."

"Old, you say?" Mother raised an eyebrow and put her finger under her chain and did what people call *knitted her brow* and said, "Old? Now *that* should narrow it down."

Considering my broken arm, I thought that she could skip the sarcasm.

"This one has brown spots all over his hands.

"Right hand or left?"

"Both."

"They all have brown spots all over both hands. Now, if this one was left-hand spotted . . ."

She was really getting me mad.

"This one's from the Ukraine," I said. I turned on the cassette and played a little of his songs. "He sang three of these before you came to pick me up. Don't you remember, he called me *Leona's son*." I must say I did an excellent job impersonating his *son*.

"Why didn't you say that you meant Mr. Malin?"

"How could I say I meant him when I didn't *know* it was him?"

"That's a *gotcha*, all right," Mom said. "Anyway, why do you want to know his name?"

"Dad liked his singing. Either his singing or his songs."

Mother smiled. "Ah! yes, the Ukraine. Why don't you come back with me tomorrow and ask your Mr. Malin to record some more?"

"He is not my Mr. Malin, and tomorrow is not your regular day."

"I know. But I got a call just a few minutes ago that Miss Ilona has broken her arm, and since her other arm is paralyzed, she has to be fed. They asked me to take care of her for supper tomorrow, and I agreed to do it."

I told her all right, that I would go, because I needed to buy a new cassette anyway since Dad wanted to save this one.

So I went.

I found the singing Ukrainian, and he told me that his name was Jacob P. Malin now, but that in the Ukraine it had been something else. When he came to this country, the man at immigration who was filling out his application wrote J-A-C-O-B just as Mr. Malin had told him to, and then he wrote P-E-T-R-O-N-O-V-I-C-H, because that is what the *P* stands for, and when Mr. Malin started telling him his last name, he didn't have room in the space for anything more than M-A-L-I-N, so they shortened his name to that, and that is what he has been ever since. He said that he has one brother named *Malinkowski* and another one named *Malinkovsky;* even though they all had the same mother and the same father, they all had different immigration officers and so they ended up with three different last names.

Mr. Jacob P. Malin sang another song for me, and I told him that I would bring him greetings from my father when I came the next day. Up to the minute I said it, I hadn't thought about going to the old folks' home three days in a row.

The lady at the front desk told me that I would find my mother upstairs, and I did. I found her sitting in a chair in front of a lady in a wheelchair. I assumed it was a woman because Mother was feeding her, and she had said that she would be feeding a *Miss* Ilona. The woman looked like a troll or one of those dolls that they make by drying an apple and letting it get all wrinkly. She had short frizzy hair on the top of her head, but it was so thin that each hair seemed to stand up like a tiny flag making claim to a quarter-inch of territory.

Mother said, "Phillip, this is Miss Ilona," so I knew that I was right in guessing that it was a woman.

The first thing Miss Ilona said to me was, "I hope, Phillip, that you did something more interesting to break your arm than I did. I fell in the bathroom."

Maybe when people get as old as this woman was, they've gone to the bathroom so much that they don't get embarrassed talking about it. I said, "I wasn't going to the bathroom."

"I fell in the bathtub," she said.

"Oh," I added.

"A common enough accident. I would rather have broken my arm skiing with Robert Redford."

I laughed. It struck me as funny that this old person here who seemed so out of time should know about movie stars, let alone think about wanting to go skiing with them.

"He's very handsome," she said to my mother. I didn't know whether she meant me or Robert Redford. I thought she meant me. Mother dabbed at Miss Ilona's chin with a napkin. Miss Ilona continued, "I always look at a pretty face this way though: it's only half an inch away from being homely. And me, I'm only half an inch away from being beautiful. If I had half an inch less of nose and half an inch more of chin, I'd be a regular bald-headed beauty queen." She laughed.

"What kind of accent is that you have?" I asked.

"Hungarian. But not pure Hungarian. It's confused with French."

"Can I record it?" I asked.

I showed her my cassette player, and I was ready to explain to her in simple terms how it worked when she said, "A cassette? I'd love to hear myself on a cassette. But wait until I am done eating. I was taught never to talk with my mouth full."

When Mother finished feeding her, I held the microphone for her, and she said, "I am Ilona Szabo, presently known as Miss Ilona, from Budapest, Hungary, by way of Paris, France, Vienna, Austria, and New York, New York, and alive and not altogether well in an old folks' home." Budapest came out *Budapesht*.

She asked me what I planned on doing with her cassette, and I told her that I was practicing doing impersonations and that I thought that learning to do different kinds of accents would be valuable and that it seemed to me that everyone at the old folks' home spoke with some kind of an accent and that I could certainly get a lot of types out of this one place.

Miss Ilona said, "You'll probably get a greater variety of accents than of stories. The people here speak a common language. It's called boring. All except me. Come back tomorrow, and I'll tell you how being so ugly saved my life."

I asked her to tell me now, but she said no, that she wanted to think about how she was going to tell me and how much she was going to tell me. So I left with Mother and asked her to stop at the discount store on the way home so that I could pick up a couple more blank cassettes, one hour on each side, and my mother stopped without being sarcastic about it.

The following day I found my singing Ukrainian, Mr. Jacob P. Malin, and played him "Hello" from my father, and then I went up to Miss Ilona's floor. After Mother had finished feeding her, she began telling her story into my cassette, and that was all right, that was perfectly all right, except for Mother.

There was Mother standing beside me listening and smiling. To tell the truth, I would rather have her sarcastic, because if there's anything a guy doesn't need—ever—is a mother standing right beside him approving of him right out in public. What a guy needs is a mother who pretends not to notice him in public, but who acts crazy about him in the privacy of his own home or condominium.

About all I found out that day was that *Ilona* means *Helen* in Hungarian and that Hungarian means *Magyar* in Hungarian.

"You know," I said to my mother as we were leaving, "if you sign a note for me to take Bus Eighty-two instead of Ninety-four, I can get off at the corner of the home on my way back from school, and I can feed Miss Ilona her supper."

"How will you get home after that?"

"I'll walk."

She gave me a look of what you might call surprise and said, "So now that you've broken your arm, you've discovered that you have legs?"

"It happens," I said, "that it was exactly trouble with my legs that got me a broken arm. Will you write the note?"

"I'd be proud to," she said, and I glanced at her, and she wasn't *looking* sarcastic. I guess she meant it.

So the following day I went to the home after school, and Miss Ilona started telling me her story.

"I promised that I would tell you about how being so ugly saved my life," she began. "Well, it all started in Budapest. My father was the second son of a rich doctor. My grandfather, the doctor, was everybody's rich relative. At least he was the rich relative that everyone bragged about. There were some others who were richer, but their money didn't come from such nice things as making sick people well. I was the first born, and when my grandfather took his first look at me, he said to my father, 'You better educate her, Isaac, because she's never going to catch a man.' In his line of work, my grandfather had seen a lot of babies, so he knew right from the start that I was no beauty, and he knew that there was no hope that I would grow into one.

"I had two sisters born after me and then a brother. My first sister was not a great beauty, but compared to me, she was quite acceptable. My second sister was better looking than the first; she was almost pretty; and my brother was downright handsome. He had eyelashes as dark and as thick as mustaches, and he had thick, straight black hair that gave him a romantic look. It would seem that my parents had been practicing on me and my sisters and by the time my brother came, they finally knew how to make a proper-looking child.

"But if I had been born semi-pretty like my sisters, I wouldn't have been sent to the French school to be educated, and if I had not been sent to the French school at the early age I was, I would not have been able to speak French fluently and without an accent, and if I had not been able to speak French fluently and without an accent, I would not have saved my own life."

That is all I got on the first day. I couldn't coax another word of her story out of her. She said much more, but it was mostly about what I did in school and what subjects I liked best and what the world was like outside the home.

I told her about my teacher and about some of the kids in my class, and she listened with interest, as they say.

"Now, what about you?" I asked. "Tell me about your schedule."

"Oh," she answered. "Nothing ever happens among the Beige and Grays."

"The Beige and Grays?"

"Yes," she said, "everyone who lives here is either beige or gray or some other shade of boring. Except me."

"Will you continue with your story tomorrow?" I asked.

"If you come, I will."

The next day was Saturday. The school bus

couldn't drop me off at the home, but it occurred to me that old folks have to eat lunch as well as supper, so I asked my mother if she would drive me over to the home so that I could help Miss Ilona with her lunch.

"Legs work only in one direction?" she asked.

"It's a question of time," I said.

"Yours or mine?" she asked.

"Yours or mine what?"

"Your time or my time? Which is it a question of?"

"If you drive me over, it's a question of both our times. Will you?"

"I'd be proud to."

That made twice in two days that she had said that, but this time I was not too sure she wasn't being sarcastic.

She drove me to the home at eleven-thirty on Saturday.

Miss Ilona was dozing in her chair when I got there. I didn't know if I should wake her, but the nurse nodded that I should, so I did. Miss Ilona seemed glad that I did. She seemed to enjoy me more than she enjoyed her lunch. "Phillip, dear," she said, "the food here is fit only for cloven-hoofed animals."

"Maybe I can bring you something from home," I suggested.

"Please don't bother. Just your presence and your

cassette is all I expect you to carry with one broken arm. But the subject of cooking does figure into my story, and I think that now I ought to introduce you to the two things that Hungarians are proudest of. One of them is their cooking. They are very proud of it.

"If you go into fifteen of the best restaurants in New York City, one will offer French food and another Italian and another German or Chinese or Russian and so on and so forth." (She said *and so on and so forth* a lot. And it just broke me up. It came out *and zo on and zo force.* Her accent was very complicated, impossible to imitate, even for a professional, I'm sure.) "But in Budapest, if you go into fifteen of the best restaurants, they will all offer Hungarian cooking. And something else you should know about Hungarian cooking. Hungarian *fine* cooking is not very different from Hungarian *everyday* cooking. A lot of paprika. Do you know paprika?" (I nodded yes. I didn't, but I figured that I could look it up, and I didn't want to slow down her story now that she was almost started.) "A lot of paprika, a lot of onions, but good. And Hungarian baked goods are the best in the world. The French don't really understand whipped cream.

"It's important for you to understand about Hungarian cooking because it is important at a certain place in my story."

"But," I interrupted, "you said that there were two things that the Hungarians were proudest of. What is the other?"

"Their language," she answered. "You have to know something about the Hungarian language. It is unrelated to any other European language except Finnish, and people that I have known who have been to Finland are not so sure that it's related there either. It's as if when they were building the Tower of Babel, a solitary Hungarian—we are a very solitary people, you know—was working in some outside corridor, talking to no one. When God's wrath fell, the Hungarian continued with his labors longer than the others so that while most of the people left the Tower in huge families, the family Germanic and the family Celtic, the Slavs and the Romantics, the lone Hungarian stayed on. Finally, sensing that he was totally alone and altogether outside, the Hungarian left and met the Finn. But the Hungarian and the Finn soon parted, for Hungarians can never keep an ally.

"Hungary has been conquered time and time again, so there is no one in Budapest who cannot speak at least two other languages. Hungarians speak other languages to strangers so that they can speak Hungarian among themselves. It is a peculiar language, almost all consonants. I think we donated our share of vowels to Hawaii. The vowels that we do have, we put fancy dots and dashes over, just to make them complicated, too. It is a runt in the litter of languages, but we love it the way you can love only a runt. Conquerors have all thought of our Magyar language as worthless and have seldom taken the trouble to learn it. And we help them because, as I said, everyone in Budapest knows at least one other language. Hungarian remains our secret code."

"But you told me that learning to speak French saved your life. Tell me about that."

"I will," she said. "Tomorrow."

And I could not get another word out of her that day.

I had forgotten about Sunday School the next day, and I called the home and told them that I had an urgent message for Miss Ilona, and when she got to the phone (I suppose someone wheeled her there), she sounded so disappointed when I told her that I couldn't make it for lunch that I immediately told her that I would see her at supper, and I didn't even want to.

I fed her in a very businesslike manner, and she must have guessed that there were at least two other things I would rather have been doing because she got on with her story immediately.

"After I finished high school," she said, "I was very well educated and suited to appreciate good literature, mostly French, and good art, mostly French. I probably could appreciate better than anyone else in

Budapest. My looks had not improved, and my family had no hopes of my making a good marriage. There was a tradition among my people—rather common at the time—that the second daughter could not marry until the first one had, and the third could not marry until the second, and so on and so forth. So there was only one thing for my poor father to do, if he was not to get stuck for the rest of his life supporting three daughters. So he did it. He sent me away. He sent me to Paris."

At this point there is a pause in the tape because Miss Ilona was studying her paralyzed hand. "That was 1938, one year before 1939."

"Well, yes," I said. "I guess I could figure that out. I guess 1938 came before 1939, just the way that 1948 came before 1949 and 1958 . . ."

"I see, Phillip, but don't you understand why 1939 was important?"

"I guess I don't."

"Hitler," she said. "In 1939 Hitler started his war to conquer the world. And in 1939 the head of our Hungarian government, thinking that this time Hungary shouldn't be conquered again, took himself on a little trip to Germany and met with Herr Hitler and promised him—by way of showing good faith—that he would cooperate with the Nazis and pass some anti-Jewish laws."

There is another pause on the tape where you can

hear me being a little ashamed of myself. "So because you were ugly and couldn't get married, and your Father sent you to Paris, you got out just in time."

"Exactly," she said.

"Is that how being ugly saved your life?"

"That," she said, "is the first part of the first part."

"Did you like Paris?"

"Loved it. But, as you probably guessed, my one talent—speaking French without a Hungarian accent—was not considered a talent at all in Paris."

"So what did you do?"

"Well, being ugly came to my aid again. There was in Paris at that time a wealthy family who wanted a governess for their children. The father wanted a young woman of some intelligence and culture and so on and so forth, and since the father had something of an eye for pretty young girls, the mother wanted one who was ugly. I was qualified on both counts, you see. So I got the job."

"Is that how being ugly saved your life?"

"That is only the second part of the first part," she answered.

The nurse came and took Miss Ilona's tray, and Miss Ilona told me that she had nothing more to say, but that she would be happy to continue with her story tomorrow, if I would care to come back.

I said that I would.

On my way out I met Mr. Malin, and he asked me

if my father would like a few more songs. I told him I would find out, but that the songs would have to wait a while because I was busy recording Miss Ilona. He walked with me to the front door and said, "I'll sing for you whenever you like."

I said, "Okay, I'll see what I can arrange." He was practically following me out onto the sidewalk.

Over the next few days Miss Ilona did continue with her story. But there is a lot of stuff on the tapes that has nothing to do with how being ugly saved her life. I just kept the cassette playing, and the microphone turned on all the time that I fed her. I'm glad I did because when I play it back now, I can hear it all. Like the time the napkin fell off her lap.

On the cassette you'll hear me saying, "I'll get it."

Then Miss Ilona saying, "Never mind, Philip, we'll just use Kleenex."

"No, it's no trouble. Let me pick up the napkin." Then you'll hear clatter, clatter, bang. "I'll get it," one voice. "I'll get it," another. Then a thump. Then a crash. When I listen to that cassette, I see a movie of it in my mind where I reached for the napkin, and the cast on my arm bumped the tray and made Miss Ilona's fork and spoon fall to the floor, and then I reached for them and the whole tray fell over, and we called for the nurse and she came, and on the tape you can even hear the nurse being patient. It's there to hear in her voice as she kept asking Miss Ilona if she would like some *other* help with her lunch and Miss Ilona kept saying, "No, no, thanks."

There were other times when I arrived at the home and Miss Ilona would be dozing, and I would start to tiptoe away so that I wouldn't wake her, but she always woke up. And at those times she seemed especially glad to see me, and we would make good progress on her story.

"I had been governess for about a year and a half," she told me, "when the Nazis occupied Paris. Mr. Pomfret—that was the name of the man who had hired me—was sent away to a Nazi labor camp, and Mrs. Pomfret fell apart. Her total training in running a household had been in how to give orders to a houseful of servants. I am not being unkind when I tell you that she was a useless woman. I told her that I would stay on and help her if she would swear that I was her cousin and buy me some forged papers."

"You blackmailed her?"

"Of course. If the Nazis had found out that I was Jewish, my life would have been over. If I had not been there to help her, the lives of Mrs. Pomfret as well as her two children would have been over. They would have dissolved in their own tears. Mrs. Pomfret cried a lot. So we developed this strange household. I ran everything. I cared for the children, did the shopping and the cooking, made all the decisions and so on and so forth, and at the same time, I made it appear that Mrs. Pomfret was in charge and that I was merely running errands for her."

"Didn't you mind having to do everything?"

"No. It was more than a fair exchange. I was capable of doing all that I did plus a lot more, but Mrs. Pomfret was doing for me everything and the only thing she could do. She offered me her name. It was a fair exchange.

"I made up my mind that Mrs. Pomfret's children would never be as helpless as their mother was, and I took it upon myself to teach them how to do useful things like cleaning and cooking and so on and so forth. To learn to clean a house you need only to have a nose for dirt and be willing. Calloused knees also help. In order to teach the children how to cook, I had to learn to do it myself. And I did. I became quite a good cook, and considering all the wartime shortages, I also became a very inventive one, and that, too, helped save my life."

At this point in her story, I had been coming to the home for over two weeks, and I had become very good at feeding Miss Ilona one-handed. She told me that I had become adroit. Even though I had become adroit, it sometimes took us a very long time to get finished with her meal because she would ask me about my day and what I had learned at school, and some other days we had agreed to watch the same television programs, and we would have to discuss them when I came. We had mostly the same favorites. We both loved documentaries, and neither one of us could stand cartoons. So we decided that we both had excellent taste. One day she convinced me to read *The Little Prince*, and she was happy that I liked it. She told me that it was better in French, and then she laughed and said that she hoped I would always remember that she was the first snob ever to tell me that something was better in French.

Between various other discussions, I did learn that when World War II was over, Mr. Pomfret returned to Paris and once again took over management of his family. They no longer had need for her, so she planned to make her way back to Hungary.

"I left the Pomfrets in better shape than I had found them. The change in Mrs. Pomfret was for the better, but I knew it would not be permanent. With the children it was different. They were and would continue to be far more self-sufficient than when I first met them. And so was I. And, please remember, I was now competent in French cooking as well as French literature and French art and so on and so forth."

By this time I, Phillip, had become something of a celebrity at the home. Everyone knew my name and said hello to me when they saw me, and Mr. Malin, the singing Ukrainian, often rode with me in the elevator up to the second floor. When he did, Miss

Ilona would act huffy and say things like, "How is Mr. Musak these days?"

"Mr. Music," I corrected.

"I said Mr. Musak, and I mean Mr. Musak. Music is lively and interesting, and Musak is just there, but not there. It's what you get in supermarkets. Mr. Malin is jealous. They're all jealous. They think they have stories to tell."

"Maybe they do."

"Then let them tell them."

"Who to?"

"To Merv Griffin, to Mike Douglas, to Donahue. How should I know? Do you want me to continue with mine?"

"If you'll calm down," I said.

"I'm calm," she answered. "I just want you to remember that I am not a Beige and Gray."

"I'll remember," I said. "You're more of an Orange-Red."

"Why do you say that?"

"Fiery temper."

She seemed pleased with that, and she calmed down. "Where was I?"

"You were leaving France after World War Two."

"Yes. It was 1949 before I got my papers back in order and made it home to Budapest. Once I got there, I hardly recognized anything. My handsome brother had been taken by the Nazis to a concentration camp, never to be heard from again—even to this day. We can only assume that he was murdered, but without eyewitnesses, my parents continued to hope. They were old and broken, and I found them more helpless than the early Mrs. Pomfret had been. The older of my two sisters was now a widow with an eight-year-old daughter, and my younger sister had married a Communist."

"A practicing Communist?" I asked.

"The Communists had taken over the whole country," she said.

"Oh," I replied. My question had been the opposite of adroit, whatever that is.

"One thing I want to make clear to you before I have finished my story," she said.

"What's that?"

"It's not easy being a Hungarian. We've been conquered too many times. We've become quite good at it, unfortunately. We have a bad habit of taking on the characteristics of our conquerors until we remember that there is no satisfactory substitute for being a real Magyar."

"May I ask what all this has to do with how being ugly saved your life?"

"Has a lot to do with it. But," she added, "I don't like to make my point too sharply. I like to blunt it a little so that you really feel it when it penetrates."

Right there, on the cassette, you'll hear a pause,

which is me thinking about what Miss Ilona has just said.

"Besides," she said, interrupting my thinking, "everything I tell you about the Hungarians will have meaning in some part of my story. You'll have to remember what I have already told you about how the Hungarians love their own cooking and their own language."

There's a gap in the tape again, me thinking again. Finally, I said, "So where do you come in?"

"Tomorrow," she answered. "Miss Ilona likes to make a grand entrance, even if it is in a wheelchair."

I shut off the cassette recorder. I was basically annoyed, and I didn't want my thoughts on tape.

As I left the building, Mr. Malin called to me, "Phillip, Phillip! Wait up."

I did.

He grabbed my good arm. "Now, listen to me, Phillip," he said, "I'm next. As soon as you're finished with Miss Ilona, it's my turn."

"I may be living here myself before Miss Ilona gets finished," I said. I was still annoyed with her.

He cupped his hand over his ear and said, "What's that?"

"You're next," I answered.

"Me, next."

"You got it."

"Got what?"

"Ohmigod," I said, under my breath, and I ducked out the fire exit.

The next day I thought that if I went in by way of a side entrance I could avoid Mr. Malin and keep Miss Ilona happy. I found a door that looked like an employees' entrance. I was practically an employee, so I went in and climbed the stairs. I climbed to the second floor, Miss Ilona's floor, but I found that the door there had no knob; it must have had a push bar on the other side and could work only one way, so I walked back downstairs and found myself going through a laundry room. I nodded casually to the woman who was folding laundry and walked toward a sign that said ELEVATOR, and I took the elevator. It was not the elevator I usually took, and it had only one button, so I pushed that. I got out of the elevator and found myself in a hallway that I had never been in before. I went to find the nurse's station. Unlike Miss Ilona's floor or the first floor, the hallway here was quiet and empty.

When I found the nurse, I saw that she was sitting in front of a whole panel of TV screens, all of them black and white and all of them showing one variety or another of an old folk in bed. The nurse was keeping guard by way of closed-circuit TV.

I studied the panel of screens and said in my best

game show host voice, "Do these contestants under-stand that there can be only one winner in our Ma-hatma Guru look-alike contest and that . . ."

The nurse's eyes traveled from my broken arm to my cassette recorder and said, "You must be Phillip. What are you doing on this floor."

"I'm lost," I answered. "How do I get to Miss Ilona's from here?"

Both the nurse and I were instantly distracted be-cause about a million red lights began blinking on a panel in front of her, and the nurse had to flip about a hundred million switches and ask, "What is it?" about a thousand million times. She obviously had left her microphone on and every one of those stars of the mini-screen had heard that I was Miss Ilona's friend, and they all wanted to see me. They all had a story to tell, and they all wanted to tell it to me, Prince Phillip and his Magic Cassette. The nurse held a microphone out to me and said, "Would you care to say a few words to these people?"

I took the microphone from her and debated for a minute about doing my Fonzie imitation, but I de-cided that they wouldn't understand, so I played it straight. I told them, "I have a date with a singing Ukrainian after I finish with Miss Ilona." I glanced over at the panel and saw those million million lights blinking. "But," I added, "I want you to know that I am working on a plan that will enable all of you to tell your stories." Then I gave the microphone back to the nurse and asked her to please pull the plug. She did. I asked her how I could get out of there, and finally she told me without interruptions.

"You're late," Miss Ilona said.

"You're lucky I'm here at all. If the people on the fourth floor had not been bedridden, I would have been kidnapped and held for a ransom of twenty-six bedpans. Now, I want you to know, I not only have the Beige and Grays, I also have the Whites after me. Everyone has some story to tell."

Miss Ilona said, "Those old folks want to tell you about how they excelled at being a mother or a father, and how, now that their children are grown, they never come to visit them, and so on and so forth."

"What about Mr. Malin? I see him quite often, and he never complains about his children."

"Mr. Malin, the Ukrainian, who walks up here with you?"

"Yes, that Mr. Malin."

"No wonder he never complains about his children. He has none. He never got married. He was a singing troubadour. Toured all over Europe. The only people who don't complain about their children are the ones who don't have them."

"Well, I sort of promised him that I would get started with his story after you get finished with yours. If you ever finish."

"Don't rush me. I'm here all the time. It was you who was late today. Now, where was I?"

"You were up to 1949. You had just returned to Budapest and found your family very changed or missing."

"Yes," she said, "there were terrible food shortages in Budapest at that time. Everyone was hungry. Except, of course, the occupying Russians. They managed to get the best and the first for themselves. The Russians have never been short on nerve, I can tell you. They had the nerve to complain about the Hungarian cooking. 'Onions and paprika!' they yelled, as they sat down to eat. They began calling my people *Paprikniks*. The Russians put a *nik* or a *ski* on the end of most of their words.

"My sister who had married the Communist heard of these complaints, so she told her husband, 'It's no wonder that Comrade Zloty is in a bad humor all the time. He has indigestion from eating our awful Magyar cooking.' 'Yes,' her husband agreed."

I began to say something about remembering that the Hungarians were most proud of their cooking, but Miss Ilona stopped me. "My sister *pretended* to sympathize. She was only pretending because she had a plan. She said to her husband, 'I know a young man who was chef to a wealthy French family and who could move into Party headquarters and cook for Comrade Zloty. He could also train the present staff to cook in the French manner, for he speaks Magyar almost as well as he speaks French.'

"My sister meant me, of course. She cut my hair like a boy's and dressed me in a chef's uniform and presented me to her husband."

"You mean that you fooled your own sister's husband?"

"It was easy. Her husband had never met me, and besides, in a Communist country there are some things that wives never tell even their husbands, and there are other things that wives *especially* never tell their husbands."

"So did you take the job?" I asked.

"Indeed I did. And I did my job very well. I mentioned that there were all kinds of food shortages, but the Russian always got first choice of everything, and I had learned to cook under even worse conditions. I got so good at substituting that sometimes I could save enough ingredients to smuggle some out and give them to my family, including my sister who had married the Communist."

"And is that how being ugly saved your life?"

"That is the first part of the second part."

"What is the second part of the second part?" I asked.

"I had a little ceremony that I taught my Hungarian helpers."

"What was that?"

"We spit in the soup."

"You what?"

"We spit in the soup. We passed the pot around and each of us spit in the soup."

"How did that save your life?"

"It saved my soul," she said. "And that is the second part of the second part of how being ugly saved my life."

As I was leaving the building, Mr. Malin approached me. He was holding a Beige lady by the hand and pulling her along. "Phillip!" he called. "I want you to meet Mrs. Silverman. I promised her the turn after me."

Mrs. Silverman held out her hand to shake mine and I noticed a number tattooed in blue on her forearm. "Pleased to meet you," she said.

"Do you have children you want to complain about?" I asked.

Mr. Malin grabbed my good arm—he had developed a bad habit of doing that—and pulled me over to the front door. "She lost her children at Auschwitz." He pointed to his arm, the spot where her tattoo was. "In the concentration camp."

If ever, if ever, if ever I felt the opposite of adroit; if ever, if ever, if ever I needed to be able to erase what I had said out loud the way I could erase what I said on tape, I would have done it then. I walked back from the door and said, "Mrs. Silverman, please excuse what I just said."

"It's all right, Phillip," she said.

As I walked home that afternoon, I got madder and madder at Miss Ilona. If she had not put into my head the thought about Beige and Grays and people wanting to complain about their children, I would never have made that remark to Mrs. Silverman. Miss Ilona was certainly an interesting woman, but she was difficult.

I had to make it up to Mrs. Silverman. I had to figure out some way to get her and Mr. Malin recorded. And all the Whites. Maybe I could get my Sunday School involved, but I thought of Myron Pincus and Lisa Halpern, and I knew that I didn't want to get babies like him or jocks like her involved. It was better to do the Beige and Grays one at a time. Waiting their turn would give them something to do. It was better for each of them to be center stage solo than for all of them to be part of a Beige and Gray chorus. How could you ever see a little blue tattoo if everyone stood in line backstage?

When I returned to the home the following day, I told Miss Ilona about my encounter with Mrs. Silverman. She got very touchy and said, "I didn't say that everyone who has children wants to complain about them."

"That's the impression you like to give. I'll bet that if you took the trouble to find out, you'd find that there are a lot of interesting stories in this place."

"But at what cost? At the cost of being bored out of my natural skin? I told you that Hungarians have a bad habit of becoming like their conquerors. I don't want to become a Beige and Gray."

"There are parts of every story that are boring," I said.

"Well, then, I better hurry up, so that you won't be bored too long," she said.

"There's no reason for you to get insulted," I said.

"You said that there are parts of every story that are boring, so I must bore you at least part of the time."

"Let me just say that some parts of your story are more interesting than other parts."

"What is least interesting?" she asked.

"The parts about the Hungarian language and Hungarian cooking."

"But they are necessary!"

"I know that!" I said. "That's why it's important to listen to the less interesting parts."

"What parts are most interesting?"

"Where you spit in the soup. I'm in no hurry for you to hurry," I said. "There's nothing I would rather do during my broken-arm phase." She smiled, and I could see that she had returned to what is called good humor. "What really puzzles me," I said, "is why no one ever guessed that you were not a boy." (By this time I had completely forgotten that when I first saw Miss Ilona I had not been certain whether she was a Ms. or a Mr.)

Miss Ilona laughed, "I never had much of a figure."

I think that at that point on the cassette you can hear me blushing, that's how red I felt.

"Actually," Miss Ilona continued, "Hungarians are artists at deceit. Some of the greatest art forgers of all time have been Hungarians."

"I'm just surprised that the Russians never caught you. In movies they are always so suspicious."

"I was almost caught once. That was in 1953, the year that Stalin died. What saved me was that after Stalin died, the man who came to power in Hungary was a man named Nagy. *Nagy* in Hungarian means *large*, and he was that. He was over six feet tall, and for a Hungarian, that's basketball player size. He loved good food, good drink, good clothes, and so on and so forth. In short, the only thing Communist about him was his politics. After he tasted my cooking, I could have been a trained chimpanzee, and he would not have let me go. In fact, Nagy was so much a Hungarian at heart that he began to loosen up a bit on the government. He began to allow the factories to manufacture things like toothbrushes and refrigerators and so on and so forth. The Hungarians loved it. Of course, the Russians did not. So after two years they removed Mr. Nagy and put one more like their own back in. And for the next year and a half while I continued to cook up my soups inside, trouble was brewing outside.

"I told you that the Hungarians have a bad habit of becoming like their conquerors . . . but only up to a point. I will explain it to you. That is, if I won't bore you."

"How will I know if you'll bore me until I hear you?"

"All right. Let me explain it like this. The Russians said to the Hungarians, 'We want to dress you up like Russian bears. Look at all the fun you will have with these sharp and powerful claws!' So the Hungarians put on the claws and scatched out a few eyes with them. Then the Russians said, 'See what fun! Now, suppose you put on a bear skin. See how warm it is.' So the Hungarians put on the bear skin and saw how warm it was and how tough the skin was. Then the Russians said, 'Now, suppose you wear these bear teeth and learn to eat like a bear.' That's when the Hungarians became a little worried."

I nodded. "Because they love their own cooking," I said.

"Yes," Miss Ilona agreed. "But they try on the teeth anyway, and they try the bear's diet, but they get a little bit of indigestion, and I must tell you that there is no one in the world who feels as sorry for himself as a sick Magyar. So the Hungarians did not take kindly to having to eat bear food. Finally, the Russians said, 'Now that you are wearing the claws, skin and teeth of the bear, the only thing that remains is for you to learn to bark like a bear.' And that is when the Hungarians revolt."

"Because they love their Magyar language," I said.

"Exactly," she said. "And that revolt is the first part of the third part of how being ugly saved my life."

"I see how the boring parts fit in," I told her.

She smiled, looking very satisfied with herself.

"So it was that in October of 1956, the Hungarian writers—for there are none who love or need their language more—became disgusted with having to wear the Russian bear costume and make sounds like a bear. The writers organized a protest, saying that they would be Communist, but they wanted to be Hungarian Communists, not Russian ones. They wanted to bark in Magyar, not Russian, and that was when violence erupted."

"Where did the violence break out?" I asked.

"Tomorrow," she answered.

"I asked *where*, not when," I said.

As I left the home, I was asked by the receptionist

to wait at the desk for a minute, that there was someone who wanted to see me. I waited, and the nurse from the fourth floor came down.

"Listen," she said, "you've got to get someone to listen to the people on my floor. You told them you were working on a plan, and they've been asking me several times a day if Phillip has come back yet. Each of them, several times a day. That's a lot of the same question," she said. "Listen, Phillip, I beg of you, come up with something for me to tell them. I can't stand it much longer, Phillip. You've got to do for them what you've done for Miss Ilona. You've got to come up with something."

I stuffed my cassette between my cast and my chest and put my good hand on her shoulder, and said, "Don't worry, nurse, I'll see to it that it gets done."

Mother had already made the appointment for the cast to come off my arm. The doctor said that after the cast came off, I would have to do some special exercises to strengthen those muscles. I knew that I wasn't going to have time to do all of the life stories. And then it came to me in a flash. The nurse had said that I must do for the others what I had done for Miss Ilona, and I asked myself, what had I done for her? I had done for her exactly what I had done for myself. I had saved her from being bored to death. Well, once her arm was better, she could have my half of the job. The cassette-listening half.

But I didn't tell her my decision immediately.

I listened first to the rest of her story.

"You asked me where violence at last broke out in Budapest. It happened outside the Budapest radio building. The people demanded that the Russian army leave our country. As the crowds gathered there, some of the Hungarian police, wearing those Russian bear skins I told you about, fired into the crowd, and that made the crowd madder. To think that Hungarians would fire on Hungarians, that they would have already forgotten who they were.

"The writers were soon joined by students and office workers and even soldiers who suddenly remembered that being Hungarian was more to their liking than being Russian bears. Everyone began marching in the streets, carrying banners, saying, INDEPENDENCE AND FREEDOM and WE WANT NEW LEADERS and WE WANT NAGY. Remember, Nagy was the Communist who came to power after Stalin had died. The one who loved good drink, good clothes and my cooking.

"There were gatherings in every public square, and in Budapest Square itself the crowd began to pull down the statue of Stalin. They didn't get the statue down until the next day, but the effort was good." Miss Ilona looked back into herself and smiled. "Oh, yes, that was good."

"What did the Russians do?" I asked.

"They did what they always do. They gave the people some of the things they wanted. They put Mr. Nagy back in as head of the government, and they got him to plead with everyone to lay down their arms. It was a wild time in the city. Radios were blasting from all the windows. Between threats and pleas—*if you don't get back to work, we'll shoot you,* and *please go back to work and we'll forgive you*—the radios played waltzes and czardas and so on and so forth. The city was a crazy place.

"Then the Russian tanks left the city, and I knew that they were planning something awful."

"How did you know?"

"Because I recognized the tactics. Remember, I had been exposed to the Nazis. I knew that they would draw back only to be able to get a running start for their final push. I knew that if anything good were to come of it, I would have to be the one to make good out of bad, just as I had learned to make good out of ugly. So while the radios blared forth for us to return to work, I began walking. I headed west to Austria and in the lull between the time the Russians said that they would leave Hungary and the time when they actually came back in and crushed the revolt, I walked on the Budapest–Vienna highway to freedom. About one hundred and sixty thousand of us did so.

"The United States took thousands of us in, and that is how I came to America."

"Did the Russians come back into Budapest?"

"Oh, yes," she said. "Within a few days. They took Nagy prisoner and they clamped down on my poor people and dressed them all in bear suits again. And walking to Vienna is the second part of the third part of how being ugly saved my life."

"But," I said, "I don't see how being ugly saved your life this time."

"Well," she answered, "if I had not been born ugly, I would not have been me, and if I had been someone other than me, then it would have been someone else's life that I would have saved."

"I hate your story to end," I said.

"Why?" she asked. "Now you can get the cast off your arm and return to riding your skateboard."

"Now, listen to me," I said. "When I first broke my arm I was doing only one thing well, and that was feeling bored and feeling sorry for myself."

"That's two things," she said.

"You're right," I said. "The same two things you were doing. When you're feeling sorry for yourself, everything looks beige and gray. Even people. I couldn't separate out one Beige and Gray from another. Until you. Until you told me that you were ugly and that being ugly saved your life. At first I was listening to Mr. Malin and *not* listening to him at the same time. Because something in my head wouldn't make room for seeing him as anything but beige and gray. Now, I'm still having trouble sorting out the people on the fourth floor, the Whites, but I figure that that will be your responsibility. Yours and Mr. Malin's."

"Never!" she said. "They would bore me to death."

"Someone has got to listen," I said. "And, Miss Ilona, you've got to overcome your prejudice about old people. How can you ever see a small blue tattoo if you're blinded by beige and gray? Now, since Mr. Malin has use of both his arms, I'm putting him in charge of the cassette, but I'm putting you in charge of Mr. Malin."

"They'll bore me to death," she repeated. "I'll become a Beige and Gray. I told you that Hungarians always take on the habits of their conquerors."

"Up to a point," I said. "You'll remember that you're orange-red, fiery Miss Ilona, and I think that will sort of add color to the Beige and Grays. Someone's got to listen to these people, and I think it has to be you."

"What have these people got to say?"

"How will you ever find out if you don't listen?"

"They'll be boring."

"Parts of them will."

We more or less quarreled until it was time for

Miss Ilona to go to bed, but when I walked home, I walked home with her agreement that she would do it. And I walked home with something else—with the feeling that she had wanted to give in after a good fight.

Two days later when the cast came off my arm, it looked about as ugly as an arm could look. It in no way matched my other arm because it was smaller and purpler, and it looked so pitiful that I thought it was going to mew because it looked and felt as weak as a kitten. I insisted that Mother and I drive to the home to show Miss Ilona and Mr. Malin. Mr. Malin met us in the lobby, and we all went upstairs together.

Miss Ilona said, "I've got three more weeks to go before my cast can come off, but Jacob and I have already started on Mrs. Silverman's story."

Mother said, "The volunteer women would like to make duplicate copies of the tapes and keep them in the library of the home. We'd like to save these lives as part of the history of the home."

"Well, Leona," Mr. Malin said to my mother, "you can thank Phillip here for getting us all started."

"Not at all," Miss Ilona said. "You can thank me."

"Now, why is that?" Mr. Malin asked, obviously irritated with Miss Ilona.

"Why? Because Phillip paid no attention to anyone until he noticed me, and he never would have noticed me if I had not been so ugly. So you might say that my being ugly saved all of our lives."

"On tape," Mr. Malin corrected.

"Not only on tape," Miss Ilona said, "not only on tape."

I liked that. I liked ending with a beginning of the first part of the fourth part. And so on and so forth.

With
Bert
&
Ray

---

by William

If I have to start at the beginning of things, I guess I would have to start with Pa. Or the end of Pa, I should say. I had long ago heard the expression of someone being *dead drunk*. Well, that was Pa. Or the end of Pa. He died dead drunk when I was six, and that was that many years ago. Half my life ago. For a long time before he died, he couldn't get anyone to sell him any more insurance, and I can't say that I blame them. Anyway, the little bit he did have, didn't hardly pay for his funeral, and the little bit that Ma got from the Social Security didn't hardly carry us from one month to the next.

So what Ma did, after Pa had been dead for three years and we had some powerful dentist bills mounted up, was to sell off all his stuff. Wasn't any of it she wanted around the house anyways. He had hunting guns and duck decoys and all the issues of *National Geographic* back to when it was started. Pa could pitch a classic fit if anyone ever did touch his stacks of *National Geographics.* He never read the blame things, just stacked them up in a corner of the bedroom and made misery for anyone who got them the tiniest bit out of order.

Ma and I put GARAGE SALE signs up at the light poles on the street leading to our house, and people snuck around to our back door trying to get in and buy some of Pa's things even before eight A.M., the time we said we was starting. They paid right good money for some of the stuff Pa collected, the guns in particular, and even them fancy Jack Bean bottles. We was sold out before noon, and we had brought in two months' worth of dentist bills from that stuff of Pa's.

Two of the people who came to the sale were Bert and Ray, this couple who have an antique store over in the section of town called Huntington. Bert and Ray were at our sale early, and they were kinda thrilled about the duck decoys and the prices Ma had put on them. We had made them odd numbers like the stores do. We put two ninety-five and like that on them, except for the biggest one that we made an even four dollars. They didn't touch the *National Geographics* or the Jack Bean bottle collection or any of the old camping equipment, but they sure did tuck them decoys under their arms real quick and paid Ma exactly what she asked for them and gave her a card, saying that she should please to call them whenever she did another house sale. Ma took the card and said that she sure would call them if she ever did another. I was speculating about what else Ma could sell until I realized that Ma is just a timid soul who says "scuse me" to the chiffonier when she bumps into it.

Next thing I know, we are over in the Huntington section of town, having our dentist appointments, and right there on Elmhurst Avenue where we stood, waiting on the bus, there was a house that had a sign out front, a neat, lettered sign saying, HUNTINGTON ANTIQUES, *Bertram Grover and Raymond Porterfield, Proprietors.* Right up on the front door was attached another sign, a littler one, and this one just said, OPEN. Ma remembered that that was exactly the name on the card given her by the couple that had bought them decoys on the day of our sale. She took the card out from her pocketbook, and sure enough, even the style of the lettering on the card matched that what was on the sign.

"C'mon, Ma," I said, "let's pay them a visit."

"Aw, William," Ma said. "It's not nice to pay a call so unexpected."

"C'mon, now, Ma," I said. "This here is a place of business, and heck, you don't need no appointment to walk into a open business unless'n it's a dentist." I marched right up onto the porch and beckoned to Ma to follow, and she did. I pushed on the doorbell that was right next to the small sign that said OPEN.

Took a pretty minute or two for them to open the door and Ma was ready to back on down, but I wouldn't let her. I told her to stand right there by the door. I noticed that the porch was fixed up right nice with wicker chairs and lots of plants in pots. On the wicker rocker was a little sticker, white with a red border that said one hundred forty dollars and then I found another sticker on a chair that said one hundred thirty dollars. Each pot that had a plant inside it had a numbered price, too. I didn't have time to point any of this out to Ma, because there at the door appeared Ray, who was smiling and welcoming us in.

Bert was standing in the front hall, and he pointed the way into their parlor, and Ma and me sat down on this here sofa with legs so skinny they didn't look like they could hold up the sofa cushions let alone Ma and me. Bert and Ray asked us to have some tea with them, and I must say that they served it up real fine in little cups you couldn't hardly fit your finger through the handle. I put my cup and saucer down on a end table and picked up a ashtray and saw one of them little white stickers with a red border on it and written on it was some letters and then a price, twenty-five dollars. It wasn't a very big ashtray neither. I got up from that skinny-legged sofa and began to wander around their parlor, and whatever I took to picking up had a red and white sticker and some letters and some number wrote on it.

"What're these here letters for?" I asked.

Ray kinda winked at me and said that that was a big secret, that that there was their code, saying how much they paid for something. Knowing that, it wasn't too much trouble figuring things out because sitting right there on their sideboard was one of Pa's decoy ducks, and I picked it up kinda casual and saw that it said RIB, and right under that code was written twenty-five dollars. Well, I knowed that we had not charged them but one seventy-five for that there decoy. All of the decoys was marked twenty-five dollars, even though we had charged different amounts, up to four full dollars for them. I just lifted each duck sort of casual like and, remembering what we had charged, I memorized that EAB was two ninety-five, PAB was three ninety-five and UNN was four dollars even. I had already spotted RIB at one seventy-five.

Bert and Ray asked Ma if she often managed house sales, and Ma said no. Then they told her that if she ever wanted help with any, they would be happy to give it to her if she would just let them in first. Ma said she'd be more than happy to let them in first, not quite understanding everything they were asking and telling.

We left their place, and I couldn't hardly wait a minute to write down the number and the letters of that there secret code. I took the card that had our next dentist appointment reminder, and I done my figuring on it.

If EAB was two ninety-five, then E was the second letter and A was ninth and B was fifth.

So I wrote all the numbers in a row and in order and I fitted the letters with their numbers like this:

1	2	3	4	5	6	7	8	9	0
R	E	P	U	B		I		A	N

Weren't but one word could fit into all that, and that word had to be REPUBLICAN, which Bert and Ray probably were.

Thing that happened not long after that was that Ma got a call from Ray, saying that there was the contents of this house to sell. Some old lady had died, and the family that was left wanted Bert and him, Ray, to handle the whole thing, but that since they had opened their Huntington Antiques Shop, they didn't want to do that kind of business anymore. So they was calling Ma to see if she wanted to handle it. They said that they would come on over to the dead lady's house with her to help her and teach her what to do if she'd just remember that she was supposed to let them in first.

Ma said sure she'd like to help them, not even knowing what was in it for her, but she wanted to thank them for having her and me to tea. She asked Ray if I, William, could help, too. I guess she figured that I ought to since I had had some tea, too, and Ray told her yes, that certainly William could help. He told her that they would lend her one of their standard contract forms to use until she could get some of her own printed up. And Ma said thanks for that, not even knowing for sure what she was thanking for, but living with Pa for as long as she had, she had got into the habit of being thankful for just any kind of common courtesy.

The contract when it came said that Ma was to get twenty cents on the dollar of whatever money she took in from the sale of household goods.

Bert and Ray showed us how you have to go around and put these prices on everything, even old bath towels so wore out that you'd be right ashamed to hang them on a clothesline, which these people didn't because they had a clothes dryer. And I didn't think any self-respecting person would leave such a kitchen when they died. You would think that Cockroaches United was having a county convention. Ray taught Ma how to tag and mark everything, and Bert taught her how to keep track of what was sold to who and how to do the book work, and they taught me how to clear out the cupboards and drawers and wash the stuff that needed it.

Then Bert and Ray went around the house and concentrated hard on putting the prices on a silver pitcher and a cut glass bowl and other stuff from the china closet. There was also a couple pieces of furniture, one sofa whose guts was pouring out, that he consulted about in some big book called *Nutting*. "I'll just check Nutting," he kept on saying. And Ma and me, we'd smile and nod and empty the drawers and closets and clean out the roach doo-doo. Ma and me have a plum good capacity for work, which neither of us inherited from Pa, I can tell you.

It's not hard to guess what Bert and Ray bought when they were the first allowed in on the sale. That big cut glass bowl was tucked under Ray's armpit and the big silver pitcher was under Bert's almost before the door was full open.

The sale turned out real good. We cleared out that whole houseful of stuff, and the heirs were right pleased and so were Ma and me. We made two hundred forty-three dollars and thirty-eight cents for our work, and that was the start of our career managing house sales. The work turned out to be pretty good and a lot steadier than either of us would ever have guessed. When you think about it, though, people are always dying, and something has to be done with all their stuff. Even people like Pa and his *National Geographics* and his Jack Bean bottles. And house sales are most always weekend affairs so's I could help Ma most all the time.

Ma and me got so's people would call us direct and not go through Bert and Ray, and we got so's we could price things out pretty good ourselves. Just ask me what a pillowcase brings at an estate sale or what pie tins go for, and without even having to think about it, I can tell you fifty cents if not worn and twenty-five cents if not rusty.

And there's something else you learn right quick. People will buy most anything at an estate sale. Was a time once when Ma was having these bad cramps, and I was right worried about her, and I made her to take her medicine and tuck it into the bathroom cabinet while the sale was going on. Doncha know, some old lady come by and insisted on buying Ma's cramp pills, and Ma sold them to her for twenty-five cents over what she had paid for them, and she had already swallowed three. I said to Ma, why did you sell them to her, why didn't you tell her real forceful like that you needed them? And Ma answered me that the lady was giving her worser cramps just from insisting. But Ma's like that, the giving-in type. How else can you explain her putting up with Pa all those years?

And I want to say one more thing about Bert and

Ray because fair is fair. They may have helped us to price some things that they were gonna be let in first to buy, but they never did anything real bad. Like if we had had some duck decoys again, they wouldn't mark them only four dollars and then turn around and sell them for twenty-five. They would mark them just right, that is twelve dollars and a half apiece and then sell them for twenty-five. What I'm saying is this, they never gave theirselves the benefit of the doubt.

Ma and me got so's we could tell the antique dealers from the regular people, and the dealers all understood how it was with us and Bert and Ray, and we all got along pretty good because most dealers have someone who lets them in first. Ma and me got so's we could make up the newspaper ads ourselves, and we had signs painted, little sandwich boards that said ESTATE SALE, real neat and professional, that we would set at the street corners and one on the sidewalk in front of the house itself.

Ma and me even developed a little bit of a social life from our business of estate sales. We also got so's we'd have Bert and Ray over to supper at least once every other week.

They both had always loved antiques they said, but they had had other careers before. Bert was retired from the marines, and Ray was retired from the civil service; but Ma told me that you can retire from those things and still be young. I wouldn't say that Bert and Ray were young. I'd say that they were middle-aged, about what the average TV father appears to be. Each one had different specialities in antiques, and they got along pretty good with each other, except sometimes when they'd be fighting before they got over to our house, and then Ma would consider it her duty to cheer them up with her good cooking and sweet ways.

They had us over to tea about as often as we had them over to supper, and they and Ma talked on the phone a lot. Bert and Ray would tell Ma what good buys they got and what fantastic pieces they had bought or sold. As soon as something crossed the threshold of their shop, it became a fantastic piece. But I was glad that they found company with each other, and Bert and Ray provided Ma with some of the best gossip this side of *People* magazine, except all their gossip was local, not national.

Ma and me came to see how getting in first was pretty important to an antique dealer. Because the thing of it is this—the hardest part about antiques is finding them and buying them at a good price. Selling them is pretty easy except for some things and those things aren't necessarily the ugliest. Sometimes ugly sells real good. It depends on the style of ugly. After a while Ma got so's she could price out the cut glass and the silver and the furniture, too. She had gathered together a little library of books, including the famous Nutting. She didn't ever do the pricing if Bert and Ray were around and if they showed even by a quick look in their eyes that they wanted to keep in practice. Ma always let them because she told me she didn't want to hurt their feelings none, and she didn't want to give them the idea that she had forgot from whence all her new career had sprung.

A lot of dealers came to Ma and promised her things if she would let them in first, but she never even thought about it twice. She was loyal, but seeing the way she had stuck with Pa way past normal endurance, anybody'd guess that.

Meanwhile, Bert and Ray started going up North to some of them big antique shows in places like Philadelphia and Lexington. They got so they were considering taking out a ad in *Antiques* magazine, and considering the price of that magazine and how many colored pictures is in it, a person's got to be pretty fancy to run an ad in there. But them and us never lost our relationship of buyer and seller, and Ma always swooned for them over their fantastic pieces.

In the meantime while Bert and Ray were getting fancier, we were, too. Our house started changing, and for the better. We were upgrading, you could say. It started when Ma couldn't sell a set of dining room chairs unless she'd of come way down on the price, and she just couldn't. She knew they was worth what she was asking, so she decided, heck, we could use them as good as anyone, and then it happened with other things, too. We got a nice set of dishes the same way, and Ma got me a Polaroid, bought it outright at one of her sales. Surprised me with it for my birthday. We also got a Pontiac station wagon at a good price. It was left in a garage, and the lawyers said that it was to be sold as part of the contents of the estate.

In our ads we always said "contents of the estate." We never called them house sales anymore.

One day when Ma and me were invited over to Bert's and Ray's for tea they had just come back from a buying trip up to Kentucky and some other horse country, I think. We no sooner got in the front door good when Ma spotted this piece of furniture leaning over by the wall to the left of the archway that leads to their parlor. Ma went on over to it and studied on it awhile and said, "I just love your *panetière*, Bert. Wherever did you find it?"

"*Panetière?*" Bert said. "What *panetière?*"

"That there cupboard," Ma said, pointing to the piece of furniture leaning against the parlor wall.

"This'n," I said. "Ma called it a *panetière*."

Then Ma looked at the ticket and said, "I see that y'all made a good buy. A right good buy."

I glanced on down at the ticket and saw that they had paid UNNN for it which was forty dollars

American, and they had marked it up to a hundred twenty-five.

Ray came in from the kitchen just then, and Bert said to him, "It seems that we made a good buy on our *panetière*, Ray."

And Ray said, "Our what?"

"Your *panetière* right there," I said, pointing to that same cupboard leaning against the parlor wall.

Ray got real upset, and so did Bert, and they said that they didn't think it was fair that we should know their code, and I asked them how did they expect us not to know, seeing's how Ma always let them in first and knew whatever it was they had paid for whatever it was they had carried out under their respective armpits. They smiled, both of them did, but I could tell that they sorta hurried us through the tea. I peeked back in the door after we left, and I saw them pulling the tag off of that there *panètiere*, which they didn't even know they had until Ma called it to their attention.

Next week Ma had Bert and Ray over to supper and Ray announced, "Bert and I sold our *panetière* for four hundred dollars to Mrs. Sinclair, the lady who just built that big house by the golf course. She's doing everything in French, and we called her and told her that we had an authentic eighteenth century bread cupboard, and she didn't even know it was a *panetière* until we told her. She bought it like that," he said, snapping his fingers.

"Fancy that," I said, "a genuine eighteenth century *panetière*, and Mrs. Sinclair didn't even know it."

Bert said, "Well, some of these people who have big houses need to be educated in good taste."

Ma just smiled and told them how glad she was for them that they had turned a nice profit. "Well," Ray said, "it's not hard to do if you buy right and know what you're selling." Ma gave me a look that said "hush," and I didn't say nothing about they never would have thought that they had nothing but a old kitchen cupboard if Ma hadn't been reading a whole lot of books besides Nutting.

Bert and Ray were in Philadelphia doing one of their fancy shows when the call came that they would like Ma to come handle the Birchfield estate. Mrs. Birchfield was the widow of one of the richest men in town. At one time, half the town owed her money, and the other half were her relatives. Ma said that she'd be most willing to handle that estate, and we went there, the two of us, full of high hopes, expecting to find treasure like in the palace of an OPEC shah of an oil producing country.

What we found was the same old grease pool in the kitchen and the same old roaches in the cupboards, none of which were *panetières*, I can tell you. The towels and the sheets were such that Ma thought she best sell them direct to the rag man. And save! That Mrs. Birchfield had so many peanut butter jars that it was hard to believe that Peter Pan never did get old.

Ma said, "Some people just don't know how to live."

The furniture was mostly good. Ma knew that. If you recovered it, it would be right pretty. Some ancestor of Mrs. Birchfield had knowed quality and had bought it. Besides the furniture, there was a nice silver coffee urn and a brass clock that chimed and some big old china tureens and bowls that must have been what the family ate off of before Mrs. Birchfield discovered jelly glasses and peanut butter jars. Ma knew that there was some fine stuff in there even if it was all tarnished, and she was glad that Bert and Ray would be back from Philadelphia in time for her to let them in first.

Ray was in a bad mood when they got to the sale, and Ma knew it, and she tried to cheer him up by showing him the very best things first, and he bought the brass clock and a coupla tureens. Then Ma saw that he was being more cheery and she showed him this big Chinese screen that was made in four panels. Ma had found it wrapped in a old bedspread in the back of Mrs. Birchfield's bedroom walk-in closet. "I put a hundred twenty-five on this, Ray," she said.

Ray looked at it and laughed. "I wouldn't have that thing if you gave it to me. It's a piece of junk."

Ma looked at it real good and said, "I think it's something good, Ray."

Then Ray called Bert over, and they both said that they wouldn't have it even if Ma gave it to them, that they both thought it was a piece of junk. Bert added that when he was in the marines, every other sailor that hit the port of Hong Kong bought at least two of these things for his wife. After they both spoke on about how junky that screen was, they didn't seem so mad at each other anymore, and Ma looked glad that she had at least helped them to make peace with each other by agreeing over disagreeing with her.

Ma couldn't sell that screen the whole time we had the Birchfield estate sale, and when it was over, she deducted the full amount of one hundred twenty-five dollars from her commission, and she carried it on home with her and set it up in the corner of our dining room where, since our dining room was not even room-sized, she could not open it all the way.

The next day after school we carried it into the parlor and there we spread it out in front of the sofa. There were four panels, and each panel told part of a story of some Chinese ladies washing clothes and doing other dainty things. Ma said that the women were washing silk. She sure had been doing a lot of reading since Pa died and we had started in the estate sale business.

She asked me to leave the screen up, right there in our parlor, blocking our sofa. The next day when I came home from school, she was sitting on a little stool in front of that there screen contemplating it some more. "William," she said, "I got a feeling in my bones that this is something really good. The next weekend we don't have a estate sale, we're gonna carry this downstate and see if them fancy dealers down there don't want it."

"What you gonna ask for it, Ma?"

"Gonna ask five hundred dollars for it, William," she answered.

I didn't do nothing but swallow.

The next weekend we carried the screen, wrapped in a bed of old bedspreads from Mrs. Birchfield's, to four different shops and didn't anyone want it.

Come the following Monday, Ma got herself over to the library and began some more reading that didn't stop until Saturday, at which time she was more convinced than ever that what she had was something real good. So the weekend after that, we loaded the thing back onto its bed of Birchfield bedspreads and headed North this time. We visited five antique shops and one interior decorator's, but didn't anyone want it.

Had it not come up spring vacation for the sixth

grade, I don't know if I would've done the next thing. Spring vacation in the sixth grade means a bus trip to our nation's capital of Washington, D.C., and Ma was real proud that we had some money to send me. I took some pictures of that China silk screen with my Polaroid. I remembered that Ma had told me that in her researching at the library she had seen pictures of some screens like ours at the Freer Gallery in Washington, D.C. She said, though, that ours was prettier, and she thought that it might could be older.

In *my* research I found out that the Freer Gallery was part of the Smithsonian and that the Smithsonian was part of our student tour of Washington, D.C. The whole Freer Gallery was China and other Oriental art.

There was a couple of things about the Smithsonian that I didn't know, and the main one of them was that it's so big, and it's not just one building, and the third one I didn't know was that they don't ever take a sixth grade student tour to the Freer Gallery part. I don't think they ever even took a sixth grade student tour there where the school was all Chinese and Oriental. The Freer is a whole quiet building that hardly anyone goes to.

We didn't.

We went to Aeronautics and Space, and we had a buddy system. The buddy system in our school means that each person has to hold onto one other person going into and going out of places so that the chaperones had only half as much to keep track of. Now, in the buddy system at our school, they usually have a girl-boy arrangement because things stay quieter that way.

It's hard to break away from the buddy system, and much as I didn't want to cause no trouble on my first field trip ever, I felt more for Ma and how bad she wanted to know about that China silk screen. So I told my buddy Carita that I had to answer a call of nature, and she blushed, even though I said it to her gentlemanly the way I did, and I left Aeronautics and Space and dodged school buses and school groups and made my way over to the Freer.

As busy and noisy as Aeronautics and Space was, that's about how quiet the Freer was. Was about like the way you'd figure it'd be in downtown Mars.

Was a lady right up front at a desk and I told her that I had some business with the person who studied on China silk screens, and the lady smiled at me, like the smile would have been a pat on the head had she knowed me better. She asked me, "Now, what business would you be having with the curator of Chinese art?"

I told her, "I got one."

She pretended that she was looking for it in front of and in back of me, and said, "Where?"

She gave me that smile again, and I could see that

she was mighty unlikely to do business with me, so I took the Polaroids out of my pants pocket. I had put them between two pieces of cardboard so's they wouldn't get mashed on the bus trip. I spread them out in front of her on top of the desk there and said, "I might be interested in selling, and I think you might be interested in buying."

She looked at my Polaroids, and I could tell that she didn't know what it was that she was seeing, and I was beginning to lose patience. They were about to miss me at Aeronautics and Space. "Listen, ma'am," I said, knowing full well how ladies liked to be called ma'am by a accent like mine. "Listen, ma'am," I repeated, "I don't have a right awful amount of time, and I would like to talk to someone in charge of these here Chinese silk screens."

"Our curatorial staff is really quite busy," she said.

And I said, "Back to home, we have a expression, ma'am."

"What's that?" she asked.

"Why, back to home we always say that there's some folk who don't know that they're through the swinging doors of opportunity until they've got swat on their backside."

She picked up her telephone.

A lady came down the hall, a magnifying glass swinging from a chain around her neck. Her name was Mrs. Fortinbras, only don't pronounce the *s*. She looked at my pictures through that magnifying glass, and I felt real proud that someone was taking that much of care with them. She took off her glasses and then she studied on me for a while. Finally, she said, "These photographs are not entirely clear and there are fingerprints on a couple of critical places, but it looks as if you might have a very fine screen there. If you ever want to bring it in and have it examined directly, it can be arranged by our staff."

I thanked her real kindly, and I asked her to write her name on the back of one of the pictures and that is how I knowed about that silent *s*.

I put the pictures back between the cardboard and then back inside my pocket, and I said to the lady at the desk, "I'll be back."

She didn't look a bit like she was glad that I had kept the door of opportunity from swatting her on her backside.

I caught up with my group somewheres between Leonardo da Vinci and the bathrooms in the National Gallery, and I didn't tell the first person about what I had been up to. I saved it all for Ma because she deserved to know it first.

Ma was out loud happy when I gave her my news, and she stopped trying to sell the screen altogether after that. Both of us was waiting, just waiting, for something to happen, and we knew it would when school was out for the summer.

I told Ma that I thought we ought to pay the Freer a visit, and she was right surprised at how firm I was about it, but she didn't hesitate much either. She loaded us and the Chinese screen into the station wagon and drove us all the way north to Washington, D.C.

"Do you remember the name of the lady, William?" she asked.

I told her yep, that it was Fortinbras with a *s* on the end that you're not supposed to pronounce and that I had had her to write it on the back of a Polaroid.

"Good boy," Ma said.

We got ourselves to the Smithsonian, that part they call the Freer Gallery, and Ma, she found herself a parking space that wasn't too awful far so's we could walk it. We marched us up to the desk there and asked to see Mrs. Fortinbras right off, and I handed the woman, who was a different one this time, the Polaroid with the name writ on the back so's there'd be no mistake about who it was we wanted and so's to cut down on the delays.

The woman behind the desk asked what was it about, and I said, "Same thing's as is on the other side of that there picture. Mrs. Fortinbras and I talked about it last spring."

She asked Ma and me to wait, and she got on her telephone, and we waited for only near a half-hour before Mrs. Fortinbras came on down the hall, still wearing that magnifying glass on a chain around her neck.

I said, "Hey," to her and she said, "Hello," back and then I said, "This here is my ma," and Mrs. Fortinbras stuck out her hand for Ma to shake it, and Ma did. Ma shook it real good.

First thing Ma said was, "We brung the screen."

"Where is it?" Mrs. Fortinbras asked.

"In the wagon," Ma said. "Should we of carried it in?"

Mrs. Fortinbras said, "Suppose you drive your wagon over to the delivery entrance, and I'll have our men bring it to one of the examining rooms."

Ma said, "Shucks, I lift heavier than that any time I do a estate sale. William and me'll just carry it on over from the parking lot, seeing's that I found a good spot not too far from here."

Mrs. Fortinbras said that they'd let us put the wagon in the employee lot if we drove it around like she said to do.

So we backed the wagon on up to the delivery, and two men came and lifted out that screen that was resting in its bed of washed bedspreads from Mrs. Birchfield's, and that made us feel that already it was important, just like Ma had thought all along.

We went along with the screen to the examination room where Mrs. Fortinbras was waiting and where the two men lifted it onto a examination table. Mrs. Fortinbras said that she would do the examining of it her own self. Ma and I sat around and waited while Mrs. Fortinbras went over the thing with her magnifier, and then she turned to us and asked would we leave it with her for a few days so's they could run some tests, and we said, "Sure." Came time for us to sign a receipt that we had left it of our own free will, and Mrs. Fortinbras asked us what valuation we put on it, for insurance purposes, and Ma said, "Ten thousand dollars." For the life of me I don't know where she come up with that figure since all's we paid was REBNN, that is, a hundred twenty-five.

We decided to leave our wagon in that employee parking lot all day and use our time for me to show Ma all the things that had been showed to me in the spring. And that Ma is a real good appreciator. She said to me, "You know, William, I do think that had I been city born, I might could get a job in one of these here museums. I think I could of. I got some real delicate feelings about some of these here things." And it would make you sad to think of Ma wasted in our little old town until you saw Ma's face as she looked at the things in the museum. That face just had to make a person happy.

We drove on back to our motel, and we looked for any messages, but there wasn't any. And the whole next day, too, there wasn't. We didn't sit around waiting. We went to visit at Congress and take a tour of the White House.

The third day we couldn't decide should we call over at the Freer or wait one more day when a call came right through to our room. It was Mrs. Fortinbras. She said that she was making a recommendation to the Museum that they buy—she said purchase—the screen at the price what Ma said, ten thousand dollars.

Want to know what Ma said? She said, "Since I been waiting here, Mrs. Fortinbras, my customer back home said that he would double his offer. So's I'm afraid I'll have to ask twenty. Thousand, that is." That's what Ma said, cool as well water.

Mrs. Fortinbras talked over the phone some more, and I heard Ma saying, "I'll do that, Mrs. Fortinbras. Sure, I understand."

I was dancing around the room, that's how anxious I was to know what was going on.

When Ma hung up, she told me that Mrs. Fortinbras said she needed a written offer from her customers back home.

"Yeah, Ma," I said. "Who might that be, seeing's how we couldn't peddle the thing for a even five hundred?"

"Why, Bert and Ray," Ma answered. "I'm sure if I call them, they'll come up with a written offer just like Mrs. Fortinbras needs."

"What do you think we have there in that screen, Ma?"

"Some genuine Chinese painting done along about the time that Marco Polo went to China. You know Marco Polo, William?" she asked.

"Sure," I said. "But I can't remember when he went to China."

"Long about the year 1260," Ma said. "I been doing some reading."

When Ma put a call through to Huntington Antiques, Bert answered the phone, and Ma told him pretty quick what it was she was calling about. And the first hint I had that Bert wasn't too happy about Ma's getting into the museum and all was that he said that he wasn't sure he could send her a written offer because what if the government held him to it. The Smithsonian was a government affair. Ma said that gosh, she hadn't thought about how the Smithsonian was a government affair. I took the phone from her and said to Bert as how he was making his promise to Ma, not to any government, and he oughtta know Ma wouldn't hold him to no twenty-thousand-dollar promise. He kept on saying "government," and I kept on telling him that it was between him and Ma, and he could ask Ralph Nader if'n he didn't believe me. I wouldn't let go—even though it was long distance—'til he got my point. Finally, he said he'd send Ma a offer in writing saying he was dying to pay twenty thousand dollars for the Chinese screen. Ma took the phone back and said to him that he should send a telegram. She said that she would pay him back. She figured it'd be cheaper than living in the motel, which was right expensive.

We got the telegram and carried it on over to the Museum, and Mrs. Fortinbras told us that the committee that decides whether or not to buy things wouldn't be meeting until early next month. Would Ma mind leaving the screen? Ma asked was the Museum considering matching the offer we had from Huntington Antiques, and Mrs. Fortinbras said yes, it was. They were prepared to pay twenty thousand dollars for the screen, and Ma said that that being the case, she was prepared to leave it for them to look at some more.

We got a telegram from the Museum when we'd been back home eight days. It said that the committee had voted to purchase the Chinese silk screen and please to send them a bill and please to keep quiet about it until the Museum itself made the announcement. I just pretended that I hadn't even read that last part of the telegram, and I called up the newspaper and told them, and a writer from the newspaper came on over to the house and listened to Ma's story and published two of my Polaroids besides, not even complaining that they were a little out of focus or that they had fingerprints on them in the wrong places.

We must have got a hundred phone calls the day that story came out in the paper. There was people who had umbrella stands and others who had statues and some who had paintings, but all of them was sure that they had themselves a museum piece and would Ma please to come on over to their place to look at it. One lady told Ma she would love to have her to come over and look at a Rembrandt painting she wanted to sell except she couldn't tell Ma who she was because she had to keep it a secret so's she wouldn't get robbed. Ma said she understood.

I told Ma that what I couldn't understand was why Bert and Ray hadn't called us up to congratulate us. A lot of other dealers had. Ma said that she understood why they had not, and she was feeling pretty sad about it.

I asked Ma if she thought that they was jealous about the money, and I reminded Ma that she had offered the screen to them first for a hundred twenty-five. Ma said that the money was just a little bit of it. "What do you suppose is the big part of it then, Ma?" I asked.

"It's hard for me to know the words for saying it, William," she said. "I know what it is that's bothering them. It's the same thing that bothered them about the *panetière*, but I don't know the psychological words for it."

Bert and Ray finally called the next day, and I

heard what Ma told them. Ma said, "It seems like I got took pretty good, Bert. I found out that that there screen I sold the Museum for twenty thousand dollars was really worth twenty-five thousand. Guess I just still got a lot to learn."

Well, that was it.

Bert and Ray come on over to the house that night and teased Ma about how she got took by the Freer Gallery, and Ma just laughed at herself right along with them.

Well, that was it.

Bert and Ray just couldn't stand being beat out by Ma, who had been their student just a few years ago. Bert and Ray couldn't stand that Ma already knew more about antiques than they did, not only because she studies on them, but also because she's got all these delicate feelings about things that you can't hardly help but notice when you watch her looking at something or touching it so gentle.

But Ma's been so wore down by everything, including living all them years with Pa, that she figures won't nobody love her if she shows that she knows one thing more than they do.

But I look back on how good she stuck by her guns with that screen when all them dealers and one decorator laughed us out of their shops, and I figure that if she can stand by her guns with strangers, she soon will be able to with people who have us over to tea.

And I figure that I got six more years before I finish school and have to go off and leave her, and I'm going to work on her. I pushed her up them steps to Huntington Antiques, and I got her to go to that Freer, and I figure that I can help her to find out how being grateful to Bert and Ray is something she should always be, but outgrown them is something she already is. By the time I leave home, she's gonna be ready to face that fact and live with it. She'll need it, being's she won't have me around to push her here and there anymore.